The Brothers Geek in

PSYBOLT
UNLEASHED

authorHOUSE®

AuthorHouse™
1663 Liberty Drive
Bloomington, IN 47403
www.authorhouse.com
Phone: 1-800-839-8640

First published by AuthorHouse   02/09/2011

ISBN: 978-1-4567-3810-5 (e)
ISBN: 978-1-4567-3811-2 (hc)
ISBN: 978-1-4567-3812-9 (sc)

Library of Congress Control Number: 2011902504

Printed in the United States of America

Villains

In the world of heroes, the most important part of the story is the villain. The villain can either make or break the story. You can't think of Superman without thinking about Lex Luthor. *The Dark Knight* was such a financial hit, in part, because of a brilliant performance by Heath Ledger as the Joker. Magneto could even be seen as a borderline hero as he is considered the Malcolm X to Professor Xavier's Martin Luther King.

In my humble opinion, one of the greatest television villains of all time is Benjamin Linus (played exquisitely by Emmy winner Michael Emerson) from *LOST*. Ben displayed the most important trait of a villain. The best villains believe what they are doing is the right thing. Ben lied, manipulated and killed, but he believed he was doing it all to protect the Island. In a well-known scene from *LOST*'s second season finale, Michael Dawson, one of the Oceanic 815 survivors, said to Ben and his followers, the Others, "Who are you people?" Ben's response? "We're the good guys, Michael." And he believed that. Ben was so effective that he had thousands of *LOST* fans agreeing with him. Being able to justify their actions, even the most repulsive and criminal behavior, is a key component to creating a villain that is more than just a cardboard cut-out.

As stated by film reviewer Roger Ebert in his review of *Star Trek II: The Wrath of Khan*, "*Each film is only as good as its villain. Since the heroes and the gimmicks tend to repeat from film to film, only a great villain can transform a good try into a triumph.*"

On the television program *Twin Peaks*, the killer of Laura Palmer was her father Leyland. But that was not all. A spirit we came to know as Killer Bob possessed Leyland. Killer Bob was a creepy looking villain whom I loved. Infused with Ray Wise's performance as the possessed Leyland Palmer, the pair was a hoot to watch.

American Sci-fi author Ben Bova wrote in his *Tips for Authors*: "In the real world there are no villains. No one actually sets out to do evil. Fiction mirrors life. Or, more accurately, fiction serves as a lens to focus what we know of life and bring its realities into sharper, clearer understanding for us. There are no villains cackling and rubbing their hands in glee as they contemplate their evil deeds. There are only people with problems, struggling to solve them."

Not all "villains" would be considered evil. Villains are the antagonist in a story, and perhaps they are just characters with character traits considered negative. Major Frank Burns from *M.A.S.H* was an antagonist for Hawkeye. He was the opposite of Hawkeye in many ways. He was a poor surgeon, had little compassion for the people around him, blindly supported the war and his country, and was portrayed as mean-spirited and greedy. Frank, however, had human traits as well. He was lonely. He was in an unhappy, loveless marriage. He wanted to be liked. Frank had a sad life, and it makes sense that he would become such an unlikable character.

In *Dr. Horrible's Sing-A-Long Blog*, the villain Dr. Horrible was actually the star of the show, and for all intents and purposes, was the show's hero. The "super hero" in the show, Captain Hammer, was the de facto protagonist. It was the classic story of how a villain becomes a villain.

And the retribution of a villain can be a powerful story. Darth Vader was the epitome of evil in the first *Star Wars* movie, but we began to learn more about him as the original trilogy progresses. We found out that he was a former Jedi who was enticed by the "Dark Side" of the Force, and he was actually Luke Skywalker's father. Thanks to Luke, at the end of *Return of the Jedi*, Vader's soul was saved.

In *Toy Story 3*, we were introduced to the only villain to ever have smelled like strawberries. The teddy bear known as Lotso is the best Disney villain ever because Lotso had real reasons for his actions. He believed he was deserted and replaced by his kid and those feelings changed the loveable, huggable bear forever. Whereas many Disney villains are basically evil because they are evil (*Snow White's* Wicked Stepmother, Gaston from *Beauty and the Beast*, *Aladdin's* Jafar and Cruella De Vil of *101 Dalmatians*), Lotso is more real, and his evil actions are so much more understandable because of this.

Of course, the following villains make their stories better with their evil and their immoral efforts to make the heroes suffer, and I wouldn't have it any other way. So thanks to the following: Dr. Doom, Jaws, The Joker, Magneto, Tony Almeda, Charles Widmore, Boba Fett, Chairface Chippendale, President Charles Logan, Helena Cassadine, The Really Rottens, Captain Barbosa, Audrey II, The Smoke Monster, Cigarette Smoking Man, Sylar, Kurt Angle, Riff Raff, Count Dracula, Megatron, Vizzini, Johnny Quick, Dale the Whale, Beetlejuice, Barry, Witchy Poo, Boris Badenov, Dr. Evil, The Fly, the Mummy, Simon Cowell, Lord

Humongous, Godzilla, Dark Phoenix, Lord Voldemort, Gorilla Grodd, The Borg, J. Jonah Jameson, Mr. Burns, Norman Osborn, Norman Bates, Wendigo, Predator, Maestro, Scrappy Doo, Sauron, Flukeman, Ozymandias, Casanova Frankenstein, Victor Frankenstein, Sweeney Todd, Thanos, Glory, Agent Smith, Andy Kaufman, Goldfinger, Count Rugan, the Skrulls, the Aliens, the First, Thrakkazog, Prince Charming, Chris Jericho, CM Punk, Captain Cold, Juggernaut, Mr. McMahon, Prince Humperdinck, Mystique, "The Million Dollar Man" Ted Dibiase, Sideshow Bob, Gentleman Ghost, Mister Sinister, Sabretooth, J.R. Ewing, Q, Natasha, Loki, Doctor Octopus, Galactus, Catwoman, Venom and Professor James Moriarty

If you do not recognize some of these villains, you should Google them. They are worth the time.

Contents

Prologue One Year ago

The small, shadowy room was private… isolated… away from the noise and the hustle and bustle of the active hospital. It was perfect. The bed clogged the room allowing only minimal movement to and from. The nurse would make her rare appearances to make sure the patient's condition had not changed… which it hadn't for the last two months. The doctor showed up even less. The medical staff was being well compensated to provide a modicum of service.

The patient did not require much aid. The massive brain injury had resulted in a permanent vegetative state. His light gray eyes opened and closed, and every once in a while his pale white leg would twitch by reflex. These were not signs of recovery, just signs of the status quo.

The curtains in the room were pulled tightly shut preventing the sun's painful rays from striking his helpless body. The sun had always been his genetic adversary, something he had dealt with since his birth.

The light from the corridor crossed the patient's pure white face for a moment as the Scot entered the room. His recently shaved head enhanced the scars around his temples; the scars from the process that had saved his life and changed it forever.

Looking down upon the albino, Anthony Randolph stood by the bedside.

"Hello Diego," Randolph said, peering at his bed-ridden friend. "Me heart breaks at seein' ya like this. Ah owe ya so much. Me life. Me health. As I stand here, I can't help but think 'bout t'irony of this situation."

Randolph turned away from the bed and moved to the window, brushing the curtains aside. He stared out the window across the Scottish horizon at nothing in particular.

"Dae ye mind him when ah was entombt in thae bed? Me body injurt an' me mind slowly dyin'? An ye were wi' me. Gazin' a' me wi' they bloody gray eyes," Randolph said.

1

He reached into the interior pocket of his black leather jacket, removing a pair of blue latex gloves.

"An' ye never gave up on me," Randolph said, snapping the gloves onto his hands. "Ye saved me life, and ah'll never forget it, brotha."

Randolph tenderly pressed his index finger and middle finger of his right hand against Diego's forehead and his thumb and pinkie against his temples. The bald Scot's eyelids fluttered rapidly as his eyes rolled back into his head. The surge up through Randolph's fingertips was nowhere near typical, though that was expected. There wasn't much of Diego left in this body.

"Thank you," Randolph said.

With a violent jerk, Randolph yanked the oxygen mask off the white face, and he cupped his hands immediately across his mouth and nose, cutting the flow of air into the comatose body.

The pressure applied by Randolph's tense muscles caused Diego's eyes to reflexively open. The gray eyes held no recognition or comprehension of what was happening, and the movement of his arms and legs was the body's natural physical response to the negative variable introduced to the situation. It was not a mental choice by the albino to thrash against the assault… it just happened.

Randolph coldly clenched his jaw firmly, his eyes piercing… focused on his intention. Veins protruded from his neck as he exerted more force. A modest smirk cracked his fixed lips as the sensation of a life slowly expiring seeped through his fingers and up his stiff arms. The intoxication of power over life and death delighted him as the buzz of the heart monitor broke the silence. Randolph ignored the sound so he could be sure that the result of his actions had been accomplished. The feel of the newly limp body beneath Randolph's heavy grasp answered any lingering doubt.

Turning his attention to the equipment in the room, Randolph silenced the buzz, and he moved back to stand beside the lifeless husk. There was no sense of urgency at the potential threat of being caught by the facility's staff. He knew that was not a concern. They'd been dealt with.

"Goodbye, Diego," said Randolph.

The cold-blooded killer reached his latex-covered hand across the eyes of the albino so the gray eyes were shut, never to open again. Breathing slowly, Randolph attempted to quell the pulsing tide of adrenaline throughout his body. He had to manage the excitement of the moment he had prepared for the past four years. Randolph allowed himself an instant of satisfaction to wash over him like the cold waves from that fateful night on the Scottish shore, but he could not allow his master's demise to overshadow his own urgent need.

He had to find him. The one whose existence made Diego expendable. The Conduit. Walking to the door, Randolph paused and glanced back over his shoulder at his handiwork. *Freedom*, he thought as he departed, leaving that chapter of his life behind him forever.

Chapter One

Starting Anew

"Danger, Will Robinson! Danger"

-Robot

Lost in Space (1965)

Parker's Point High School

In the hallway outside the office

Monday, 8 AM

"Are you guys finally done? It's about time," said Westley, standing up from the ledge where he sat and waited.

Nyx and Nigel Grimm exited the office. They had been putting their computer skills to work trying to secure the school's computer system. It was a punishment, but as punishments went, it wasn't too bad. Of course, it meant that the boys had to get to school really early to accomplish anything.

"Jeez, it's been forty-five minutes," complained Westley, whose computer abilities paled in comparison to his brothers'.

"No one said you had to come along," Nigel, Westley's twin, said. "It was your own decision."

"Yeah… well," muttered Westley. He didn't want to walk to school by himself. He hadn't really wanted to be alone lately so Westley had decided that earlier was the better option.

"Knock it off you two," said Nyx.

Nyx was the oldest of the Grimm brothers, a sophomore. The three of them had become known as the Brothers Geek. Although Nyx still wasn't flattered by the epithet, he had stopped cringing every time he heard it. On the other hand, Westley and Nigel were considering having t-shirts made.

"How much longer do you guys have to work in the office?" Westley asked.

"I don't know. I guess until Dad says so," Nyx said, knowing that his father and the vice-principal Mr. Stanton had cooked this up together.

"Ugh… who knows how long that could be," bemoaned Westley.

"Stop whining Westley," criticized Nigel. "You sound too much like Luke Skywalker… whine… whine… whine."

"Luke was a Jedi Master!" exclaimed Westley, defensively. "He's no whiner!"

Strange. Westley's not offended by being called a whiner, thought Nyx as he shook his head in disbelief. *Luke Skywalker being called a whiner, though, offends him.*

"But I was going into Toschi station to pick up some power converters," quoted Nigel in the whiniest voice he could muster. "Uncle Owen, this R2 unit has a bad motivator!"

"Stop it!" Westley insisted.

"It just isn't fair. Oh Briggs is right. I'm never going to get out of here," continued Nigel, undeterred. "That little droid is going to cause me a lot of trouble."

"Nyx, make him stop!" Westley said firmly and full of insistence.

"That's enough, Nigel," said Nyx. *If I had a dime for every time I...* Nyx was unable to complete his thought as Nigel interrupted his train of thought.

"Hey, are you going to Bright's tomorrow?" Nigel said, as if the previous few seconds hadn't happened.

"Duh!" Westley said. "Tomorrow is new comics day... of course he's going."

Bright's Comix was the local comic shop, but it was much more than that. The shop was a front for the owner, Max Bright. Max had come to Parker's Point for a reason. He had come to find the Conduit.

"Besides," continued Westley, "Nyx probably has mumbo jumbo to do with Max."

"Yeah... that's what he gets for being *the Conduit*," taunted Nigel, contorting his face toward his older brother.

"Nigel!" Nyx said sternly. "Keep it down."

"Nobody's going to hear me... and if they do... nobody's going to understand me," Nigel said.

"Even still," Nyx said in retrospect, unsure if telling the twins the truth was a good choice. "We have to be careful. Max told me that no one else could know."

"Secret identity, we got it, Nyx," said Nigel, rolling his eyes. He had been reminded multiple times by his brother. "Although, how can it be a secret identity if your arch nemesis knows about it?"

"He's not my arch nemesis," Nyx contradicted. Nyx knew exactly to whom Nigel was referring.

"Venom knew Spider-man's secret identity and that worked fine," said Westley. "And so did Norman Osborn."

"Ah... who *didn't* know Spider-man's secret identity?" snapped Nigel.

"You can't compare real life to comic books," Nyx said. He was surprised by those words coming out of his mouth.

The twins gasped nearly simultaneously.

"Heresy!" Nigel blurted.

"You don't mean that, Nyx," Westley said, like he had been wounded to the core.

"Sorry," Nyx apologized realizing his error immediately, and Nyx felt about three inches tall. "I wasn't thinking."

"You **should** be sorry," said Nigel.

"Yeah," Westley said, "words can hurt."

"Heads up… there's an Uber Geek sighting," Nigel said, pointing down the hall.

Julian Oswald, or the Uber Geek to the twins, had become Nyx's first friend after the Grimm family moved to Parker's Point. That was until Julian was proven to have stolen money from the football team in order to set up starting quarterback Noah Ridge. Julian was after Noah's girlfriend, Penny, and his plan to frame Noah was uncovered by the Brothers Geek. The friendship was fractured. Julian then kidnapped Westley and tried to use him as a way to manipulate Nyx into doing what he had wanted.

Directly behind Julian was Parker's Point High School's new counselor Anthony Randolph. Mr. Randolph had volunteered to mentor Julian after his brush with the law. Mr. Randolph had said that he was going to take Julian under his wing and, as he said, "show him the error of his ways." Those words had worried Nyx. He knew some background information on Mr. Randolph that wasn't public knowledge.

"Well, well," Julian said, snidely emphasizing the phrase. "If it isn't the Brothers Geek. Walking around like you own the place."

Julian's reputation had changed practically overnight since the incident. He went from a rarely seen geek to a bad boy with an edge. There was an air of danger surrounding him now. It helped that he was the son of the city's mayor and one of the top cardiac surgeons in the state. There was some power and wealth behind the scenes for the Uber Geek.

"Julian," Nyx said, in a restrained, yet polite voice. Nyx did not want a confrontation with his former friend and his upbringing shone through.

"So Mr. Grimm, how goes yer project for Mr. Stanton?" asked Mr. Randolph

Is his accent changing? Nyx thought. Mr. Randolph's accent had softened quite a bit since his arrival despite not being here that long.

"Fine," said Nyx, not really wanting to engage the counselor in a long discussion either. Brevity was something Nyx craved at this moment.

"Well, glad to hear it, laddie," Randolph said, placing his hand squarely in Julian's back. "If ye would excuse us, Mr. Grimm…"

Nyx kept his eye on them as they continued down the hall and turned the corner out of sight. He anticipated trouble from those two.

"See you, Nyx," said Nigel as he and Westley headed toward their first class of the morning. The hallways were becoming fuller as more of the student body was arriving for school. Nyx was about to go to Mrs. Templeton's science class when…

WHAM!

The sound of metal denting cascaded down the hall, startling several of the students. Nyx knew that the sound had come from the hallway that Julian had just gone down. Though curiosity filled his heart, Nyx didn't really want to get involved. He had had enough involvement with Julian and his problems.

"Nyx!" said Mandy, as a small, thin girl ran over to him.

Amanda "Mandy" Short was a sophomore who had been seated beside Nyx in Mrs. Templeton's class. Because science was an interest to both of them, Nyx and Mandy had struck up a friendship.

"What was that noise?" Mandy asked as she brushed her straight, shoulder-length, brunette hair behind her ears.

"I don't know," Nyx said, though he suspected. "Let's get to class."

Mrs. Templeton's room was found at the far end of the hall, which required Nyx and Mandy to walk past the corner. Trying to move quickly, Nyx nonetheless was unable to resist the temptation, and he took a fleeting look down the passage.

Julian stood, fists clenched, in the center of the hallway, his face bright red. Mr. Randolph was positioned to Julian's left, and he was glaring at the back of his head. A slight twitch throbbed beside the eyebrow piercing on Mr. Randolph's forehead. Neither was talking and the other students in the hall moved past as if nothing strange had happened. Julian saw Nyx walk by.

"What's that about?" asked Mandy as they moved away from the corner.

"I don't think I want to know," said Nyx, though he was concerned that what he wanted wouldn't matter.

Nyx and Mandy arrived at the science room with plenty of time to spare before class started so they sat down at their table. Mrs. Templeton was busy watering the plants scattered throughout the room. She had quite the green thumb as other teachers would bring her plants that were brown and frazzled, and Mrs. Templeton would, without fail, nurse them back to health.

"Good Morning, Nyx, Mandy," Mrs. Templeton said as she was filling up her little green watering can.

"Morning," Nyx said, getting out his science folder from his trapper. Nyx was into the world of techno-science more than botany, but he appreciated Mrs. Templeton's passion on the topic.

"Nyx, can you help me with the geometry assignment?" asked Mandy, pulling out her geometry textbook and laying it on the slick, black tabletop. "I don't get it. It's so hard and I know…"

Mandy's words trailed off as the science room, normally filled with so much natural light, was engulfed in darkness from out of nowhere.

Nyx looked around the classroom quickly, trying to see Mandy or Mrs. Templeton, but they were lost in the ebony darkness. Nyx knew what this was. This was not the first time this had happened.

Prophesight, he thought.

Nyx was a little surprised by the sudden appearance of the Prophesight. He had convinced himself that he would need to be, like the last time, at Bright's Comix for the *connection* to be made. He wasn't sure why he had thought that, but obviously he had been incorrect. Here he was… in first period science… and the swirling darkness surrounded him once again.

Prophesight was a force in the universe created from energies generated by psychics, mystics, witches, and other magic users as well as other paranormal acts. The Conduit was able to receive messages from the source that could lead to the prevention of terrible tragedies.

A streak of bright white light sliced through the darkness flashing directly beside Nyx. The boy covered his eyes to protect them from the pain of the sudden shine. When he opened his eyes, a lone figure stood before him, aglow like a star in the late night sky.

The figure stood stoically, silently. His long, thin, white hair masked his pale face and partially obstructed his soulful, gray eyes. The man was cloaked in a silver robe, which made his withered frame look sturdier. He just stood there, staring at Nyx.

"Um… hey," said Nyx, a little uncomfortable, feeling like an animal on display at the zoo. "What's up?"

The mysterious figure made no effort to respond as he continued to stare at Nyx.

"Do you have some kind of message for me? Am I supposed to help someone else?" asked Nyx, remembering the last time.

The figure remained silent as the grave. Deathlike. The eeriness was getting to Nyx as the surreal experience frightened him.

"What is it? Please say something," said Nyx, a distinct quiver appearing in his voice. Trying to keep himself grounded in an area that he was comfortable with, Nyx continued, "Are you the *Spectre*?"

The humor was lost on the figure, and Nyx quickly dropped the comparison. Finally, the figure raised his long, thin, right arm and pointed his completely white fist toward Nyx, extending his index finger. The mouth of the man moved, but no sound came.

"What was that?" Nyx said. "I didn't hear you. What did you say?"

His lips once again moved, slower this time, and Nyx realized that the man could not speak. If there were a message to be discovered, Nyx would have to get it in a different manner.

Nyx watched carefully as the man's lips moved with intent and with predetermination. He had never tried to read someone's lips before, but the man was making it as easy as possible.

"Danger?" Nyx said, after a moment of focusing upon the white lips. "Who's in danger?"

The figure points at Nyx for a second time and the message had been delivered.

"Nyx! Nyx!"

The sound cleared the darkness from the room as Nyx blinked several times, and his head snapped back. Mrs. Templeton leaned on the table beside him, with her hand on Nyx's shoulder. Mandy's white knuckles gripped the back of her chair, supporting herself with it. Fear and confusion could be found within her brown eyes.

"Nyx, are you alright?" Mrs. Templeton asked.

"What?" Nyx said, still not quite out of his stupor.

"You're sweating," said Mrs. Templeton, "and you're all clammy. What happened?"

"I... I... don't know."

Mandy held her breath as the fear slowly subsided.

"Mandy came and got me, Nyx," said Mrs. Templeton. "She said that you went into some kind of... trance."

"Trance? No... no... nothing like that," Nyx said, desperately hoping to hide what had just occurred.

"It was scary, Nyx. One minute I'm telling you about geometry, and the next minute you're just staring past me. It was like you weren't even here anymore," said Mandy.

"No, I'm fine. I'm sorry," Nyx said, not sure what to say.

"I think you'd better go to the nurse, Nyx," said Mrs. Templeton.

"No, I'm okay," he said.

"No, people don't just drop off like that. You'd better go see what she has to say," the science teacher said. "Please."

"Okay," said Nyx, knowing that he didn't have a much of a choice. *How can I explain this to them,* he thought, *especially when I'm not sure about it myself.*

Nyx stood from the table, stopped a moment to look at the place in the room where the white skinned man appeared with the haunting omen and shivered. Danger.

Chapter Two

The Uber Geek Strikes Back

"If you only knew the power of the Dark Side."

-Darth Vader

The Empire Strikes Back

"I'm getting tired of waiting!" Julian exclaimed, slamming his fist down on the table. "When are we going to start?"

Anthony Randolph sat at his desk and allowed the young man to rant on for a few seconds. Releasing the pent up frustrations was healthy, and this was a safe place for such an outburst. However, a few seconds was all he would allow.

"Calm yerself, Mr. Oswald," Randolph calmly said as Julian finished his tirade. "If ye remain patient, everythin' ye wish will come to fruition."

"You keep saying that but nothing ever happens," Julian spouted. "I want Nyx Grimm to pay! You promised me that Nyx Grimm would pay for his betrayal!"

"And he will, laddie," said Randolph. "Trust me."

Julian was impatient. Nyx had been his friend... his fellow geek... and Nyx had betrayed him... deserted him. Nyx had chosen the football player over Julian. It was the worst thing Nyx could have done. Julian knew something about being deserted. He lived it daily.

"When?" Julian continued to press, and he showed little sign of calming down.

Mr. Randolph placed both of his hands palm down on his desk top and slowly rose from his seat, a grimace of sour exasperation across his portrait. Julian backed away feeling the presence of Randolph's glare.

"Patience, 'tis a virtue, Julian," said Randolph. "Haven't ye heard the old phrase 'vengeance 'tis a dish best served cold?' Yer passion is commendable, boy, but misplaced and reckless. It's what cost ye the last time. Snatching the boy and tying him up. Over some girl. Foolish. Now... sit down."

Julian eased himself into the chair; the steely stare of the counselor grew sharper, the smile frozen in place.

"Sorry," Julian said.

"It's alright, Mr. Oswald. Cooler heads will prevail," said Randolph, returning to his own chair.

"Thank you, sir," Julian said, before he realized it.

"Yer welcome. Now laddie, come. It's time for ye to head to class," he said, with a short, saucy smile. "I'll walk with ye."

Julian nodded, grabbing his book bag and leaving Mr. Randolph's office. Randolph stepped out and walked directly behind the junior. They did not speak.

There was no hesitation in Julian's stride when he saw the Grimm brothers ahead of them. In fact, he had picked up his step. With an anticipatory delight, Randolph smiled inside while remaining detached on the outside.

"Well, well," Julian said, snidely emphasizing the phrase. "If it isn't the Brothers Geek. Walking around like you own the place."

"Julian," said Nyx, with restraint.

"So Mr. Grimm, how goes yer project for Mr. Stanton?" asked Mr. Randolph.

"Fine," said Nyx.

"Well glad to hear it, laddie," said Randolph, placing his hand on Julian's back. "If ye would excuse us, Mr. Grimm…"

Don't just walk off. Do something, thought Julian, biting his tongue to prevent himself from saying anything more. Julian could feel the slight force on his back increase as Mr. Randolph directed him down the hall.

"Keep yer eyes forward, boy, and hold yer tongue," whispered Randolph almost directly into the dark, mullet-like hair running down Julian's neck. He knew that Nyx was watching them move down the hall, and Randolph wanted to give him nothing to see.

The fury within the Uber Geek boiled, his face reddened, and his arms trembled with anger. Once they had turned the corner and were out of earshot of the Brothers Geek, Julian turned on Randolph like a rabid dog.

"What was that about?" Julian savagely exclaimed.

"Keep yer voice down, Mr. Oswald," said Randolph, as the other students walking in the hall or standing at their lockers stared at the unfolding drama.

"Don't tell me what to do!" Julian screamed, slamming his clenched fist into the nearby locker.

WHAM!

As the dented locker echoed through the school, the onlookers scattered immediately. However, as soon as they had started moving, the other students stopped, slowed down, and continued as if nothing had happened. Randolph stepped behind Julian who, fists clenched and beet red, was spellbound.

Yer all about instant gratification, Mr. Oswald, but the best-laid plans are those that develop slowly… that have a chance to breathe. I understand the spark… but once the flames go out, what do ye have? Ashes. Trust me and the flames will burn forever, and Nyx Grimm will never be the same.

Julian, surprised at Mr. Randolph's admission, turned his head slightly to see the counselor out of his peripheral vision.

"But…" Julian started.

Say nothing more… Randolph continued. Julian did not see his lips move. At that moment, Nyx and Mandy walked past the corner, and Julian's attention was drawn away. The former friends made fleeting eye contact until Nyx passed out of view. Julian's face turned gray as rotten meat and a snarl tattooed his craw.

"Slow burn, you say?" Julian said, squeezing a whisper from his lips, barely audible.

Aye. Ye be findin' that be more satisfactory, laddie.

"You're the boss," Julian said, turning to face Randolph.

"Yer forgiven, Mr. Oswald," said Randolph. "Ye better be gettin' to yer class."

"Thanks, see you later, Mr. Randolph," Julian said, again turning, as if to escape. This eldritch hallway encounter had left Julian both with a vague, disquieting feeling and a wonderful inner perception. And he wasn't sure why.

As Julian departed, Randolph's vacant face fissured into a smug smirk releasing a tolerant chuckle. With the intent of returning to his office, Mr. Randolph brushed through the increasingly congested hallway when his progress was given the quietus by a long absent aura and an ice-cold premonition.

Diego, he thought, as he stood, an obstacle to the oncoming student traffic like the orange cones at a highway construction site. *How unexpected. I should have anticipated this possibility.*

The overpoweringly poignant pathos directed the counselor along the path toward the science room, where the source of this disturbance originated. However, as suddenly as the feeling started, the sensation ceased as if it was never there in the first place.

The feeling's abrupt end nonplussed Mr. Randolph's senses momentarily as he strained to clear his head. He felt vulnerable, and he did not like that feeling.

"Mr. Randolph," said Mrs. Templeton as she stepped out of the door of her classroom. She had her arm over Nyx's shoulder. Nyx looked a little shaken.

"Hmmm," Randolph trailed off blankly.

"Mr. Randolph?" repeated Mrs. Templeton.

"Err... oh, I be sorry, Mrs. Templeton," said Randolph, readjusting to reality, "what may I be doin' for ye?"

"I wonder if you would escort Nyx to the nurse's office for me," she said.

"Are ye not feelin' well, Mr. Grimm?"

"I'm fine," Nyx said in a singularly mild, firm voice.

"Nyx was in some kind of unresponsive daze," Templeton said. "He seems better now, but I just want him to be checked out to be sure."

"Aye. O'course, Mrs. Templeton," Randolph said. "I would be happy to help the lad. Come on, Mr. Grimm."

Great, Nyx thought, already feeling edgy from the Prophesight. *This is just what I need.*

"Thank you, Mr. Randolph," Mrs. Templeton said. "Nyx, I hope you feel better."

"Yes, Mrs. Templeton," Nyx said, realizing that there was no way out of this.

Nyx walked toward the nurse's office with Mr. Randolph an uncomfortable step behind. To Nyx's chagrin, Scottish eyes completely covered the young geek's gait. Not usually paranoid, Nyx couldn't help but wonder why Randolph had been outside the science room in the first place. *If only I could read minds*, Nyx thought, as he picked up the pace.

"Slow down, lad," Randolph said almost laughing, "it's not a race. No need to make yerself worse on the way."

"I'm fine," retorted Nyx, wishing the man would just let him be.

"Of course ye be," he said, in a soft, reassuring voice that creeped Nyx out even more. "But ye'd be a fool to ignore the messages yer body be givin' ye."

Whatever, Nyx thought.

"Tell me about this... daze ye were in, Mr. Grimm. What happened?"

This is a nightmare, Nyx thought.

"It was nothing," Nyx said finally, "just didn't eat any breakfast this morning. Most important meal of the day, you know."

The cavalier attitude did not play well on Nyx. He just could not carry it off.

"Are ye sure that be all?" Randolph pressed.

"Yeah, I'm sure," Nyx said, confident that there was nothing wrong with him. "I'm just fine."

"I must be sayin' that ye do not seem too sick. So what do ye think caused this *daze* that Mrs. Templeton be speakin' of, laddie?" Randolph already knew the answer, but he was more interested in what Nyx would tell him... or more likely, how he would avoid telling him. Mr. Randolph knew that you could tell more about a person when they were lying, than when they were telling the truth.

"Didn't I already tell you? Breakfast," Nyx said. "Probably some low blood sugar. My mom has that same problem."

"Aye, that be common," Randolph said. *Interesting*, he thought.

As his destination came into sight, Nyx's spirits picked up as the hopes of the end of this unpleasant complication filled his head.

"Well, I'm here, safe and sound. Thank you, Mr. Randolph... I can take it from here," Nyx said, not trying to hide his relief.

"Mr. Grimm," Mr. Randolph said as he grabbed Nyx by the shoulder and prepared to drop the proverbial 'other shoe.' "I think we should take this opportunity to discuss the problems ye been havin' with Mr. Oswald."

Ugh, thought Nyx, trying not to roll his eyes.

"I have to go to the nurse," Nyx said.

"Not now," Randolph replied, smiling at Nyx's efforts to get away. "After school today... in my office. We have the chance to make some progress in the walls that have been built up around the two of ye. Ye would like that, wouldn't ye?"

"Um... I've got to..."

"Three-fifteen," said Randolph, unequivocally.

"But.."

"I'll see you then, Mr. Grimm."

Mr. Randolph released Nyx's shoulder, and Randolph's diorama of facial aspect told Nyx that skipping the meeting would not be an option.

Waiting and watching as Nyx, who peered over his shoulder at the counselor, entered the nurse's office, Mr. Randolph began his trek back to his office.

Perfect, Randolph thought.

Chapter Three

Mind Games

"I don't have to be psychic to see something's bothering you."

Professor Charles Xavier

X-Men: The Last Stand

Parker's Point High School

Mr. Fleur's American History Class

Monday, 2:59 PM

Nyx found himself in the familiar place of watching the minute hand of the clock travel around its face, counting down the seconds until school was out. Today, however, instead of the anticipation of the end of another school day, Nyx felt the trepidation of his meeting with Mr. Randolph weighing heavily on his mind.

He had left the nurse's office this morning with a glazed donut after successfully convincing the nurse that the mysterious daze had been caused by a drop in his blood sugar. Nyx had considered pretending to be sick so he would be sent home and would not have to go to see Mr. Randolph, but there were two problems with that plan. One, the nurse never sent anyone home unless they were throwing up or had a fever, usually a fever of triple digits. And two, even if he were able to avoid the meeting, Nyx would just be delaying the inevitable. Mr. Randolph was not going away, and this day would come eventually. *May as well be today*, Nyx thought, cleaning his glasses with a fluffy rag.

When the clock struck three and the bell rang, Nyx was far from the first student up and out of the desk. In fact, he was the near the end, bracing himself for what he would have to do. Standing, Nyx had to find his brothers and tell them. Nyx had intended to talk to them during lunch, but the twins weren't there. It was odd, but not uncommon. So Nyx headed to their lockers, where they met every day.

But Westley and Nigel weren't there either.

Trying not to panic, Nyx started letting his fertile mind free, concocting any number of possible whereabouts for his brothers. This was not like them. Could it be like the last time?

"Hi, Nyx," the soft female voice brought Nyx back from the edge of despair. Novella Munroe and her twin sister Jenette were heading toward the library. Nyx took a deep breath, calming himself down. *Chess club*, he thought.

The Munroe girls were in Westley and Nigel's class, and they were in chess club. It was held every Monday in the library, and Westley had been dragging Nigel with him. Nigel was always more of a fan of Risk than chess, but Westley had had a crush on Novella since they moved here. Nyx had joked that he just liked her because of her sharing the last name "Munroe" with Ororo Munroe, Storm of the X-Men, an accusation Westley denied. In fact, he denied even liking Novella, but it was clear to anyone who knew him that he did.

"Hi Novella," Nyx said, as the pretty young brunette walked toward the library. He always thought of his mother's antique porcelain dolls that sat upon her bedroom dresser when he would see these girls. They shared many qualities. They were not much taller than those dolls. Not wanting to be rude, Nyx added, "Jenette."

Jenette wasn't nearly as friendly as Novella, and she dismissed Nyx with a huff and a flick of her head, which sent her waist length hair snapping at him like a snake.

"Have you seen my brothers?" Nyx asked after dodging the flipping hairdo.

"Not lately," said Novella, "but they're probably already in the library."

"How is chess club going?" Nyx asked.

"Why do *you* care?" barked Jenette.

"Hey, I didn't mean to start a flame war," Nyx said, though neither twin recognized that term and didn't know what he was talking about.

"Jenette!" Novella scorned harshly. "Be nice! I'm sorry, Nyx. Jenette got up on the wrong side of the bed this year."

"What does he care about chess club? All he cares about are his comics and his computer," she snarled.

"I've played chess on my computer," Nyx said, hoping to smooth things over with a common interest. However, the icy glare he received revealed how unsuccessful he was.

Evil twin come to life, he thought as they arrived at the library. Nigel and Westley were nowhere to be found.

Nyx was really concerned now. Had this been a normal day, he probably wouldn't be as visibly upset, but with the Prophesight this morning... the white-skinned vision that provided the warning of imminent danger... and Mr. Randolph's weird behavior... it all added up to trouble.

Without another word to the Munroe twins, Nyx took off from the library. He hoped that he could find answers in Mr. Randolph's office. That was where everything was pointing.

The blur of the red and white paint made the hallway like a red sundown night, but Nyx wasn't stopping to see. He raced towards the guidance office aswarm with terror-stricken panic. Nyx remembered the tale Max had told him about Anthony Randolph, and those imagined horrors spurred him on.

The appearance of Nigel walking seemingly unhurt and nonchalantly out of the door of the guidance office filled Nyx with joy, as he grabbed his brother in an embrace.

"What are you doing?" Nigel said, immediately pushing his overzealous brother away. "Knock it off, Nyx. What's wrong with you?"

"Where's Westley?" Nyx said, between huffs.

"He went home," Nigel said, looking around to make sure no one had seen the hug.

"He went home alone?" Nyx asked, knowing his brother's recent aversion.

"Mom picked him up," he replied.

"But… chess club?"

"Mr. Randolph wanted to see me, and Westley didn't want to go to chess club alone. *Novella*," said Nigel, nodding a knowing smile. "We called Mom and asked her to pick him up."

"Mr. Randolph wanted to see you?" Nyx questioned.

"Yes," Nigel said.

"Why?"

"He said he wanted me to look at his computer system that he uses for his files and see if I could upgrade the speed and security," Nigel responded.

"When did he ask you to do this?"

"Earlier today. Westley and I worked on it during lunch," said Nigel.

Well that mystery's solved, thought Nyx.

"You shouldn't be alone with Randolph," chastised Nyx. "You know what he did."

"Come on, Nyx. This is school. He's not going to try anything at school," Nigel replied. "Besides, this gives me access to his computer."

Nigel smiled his troublemaker smile, and Nyx felt worried.

"We can't all be the Conduit," Nigel said, "but we can still contribute."

"Nigel!" scolded Nyx.

"Hey Nyx… we're a team. We're the Brothers Geek, remember?" Nigel said, pleased with himself.

"How can I forget?" Nyx answered, pulling Nigel away. He whispered to his brother, "I had another...message today... you know... from the Prophesight."

"Cool!" blurted Nigel.

"Shh," hushed Nyx, smacking himself with a facepalm.

"What now?" Nigel said, his voice back under control. "Another mystery? Stolen jewels? Kidnapping? *Murder*?"

"I don't know," Nyx said, ignoring the over-the-top bravado of his brother, "all I know is there is danger for us."

"**All**... right," Nigel exclaimed again, catching himself in mid-exclamation. "Tell me all about it."

"I'll tell you later... at home. Now, I'm supposed to be in with Randolph."

"Yeah, I saw that on his calendar," Nigel said.

I wonder what else Nigel saw in there, Nyx thought.

"I'm not going straight home," Nigel said. "Mom asked me if I would go and sit with Ariel at her gymnastics practice. Mom had a meeting with her agent, and then she would pick us both up."

Nyx liked that his mom was starting to put some responsibility onto the twins. *Less for me to do*, Nyx thought.

"Then we'll talk when you get back from that," Nyx said, his curiosity now piqued even more about Mr. Randolph. It couldn't just be a coincidence that he had talked to Nigel.

Nyx opened the door to the guidance office and walked inside. The large, open room had a very homey feel; welcoming couches and a wooden rocking chair arranged in a semi-circle. The light bluish shag carpet maintained its new smell and soft texture. Posted on the white walls in the room were inspirational quotes from celebrities and well known public figures ranging from Vince Lombardi to Mahatma Gandhi.

Near the rear of the room was an open door that led into Mr. Randolph's personal office. Nyx slowly moved toward it. Mr. Randolph sat behind the oversized oak desk, leaning back in his black leather chair.

Nyx couldn't believe his eyes.

A mechanical pencil magically floated in the air in front of Mr. Randolph's face. The defiance of gravity he was witnessing was shocking. As Nyx moved in for a better look, the pencil dropped from its point of levitation into Mr. Randolph's hand. Without missing a beat, Mr. Randolph tossed the pencil back up into the air, it spun, and he caught it again as it, this time, dropped immediately. There was no sign of the pencil "floating" now.

Mr. Randolph turned to Nyx, and he did the "David Letterman pencil trick" once more. It was as if he was trying to make it look like this was what he had been doing the entire time. Nyx didn't buy his sell job. Nyx knew what he had seen.

"Ah, Mr. Grimm," Mr. Randolph said, "ye be late."

"Yeah, I couldn't find my brothers," Nyx said, sitting at the rectangular conference table.

"Young Nigel was here. Ye shoulda come here immediately. Ye wouldn't have been worried," Randolph said, placing the pencil into the can on the desk. Upon the can, glued in place, were a variety of pictures of eyes taken from magazines. There were plenty of eyes that Nyx recognized… Robert Downey Jr., Bruce Willis, Megan Fox… to name a few. The majority of the eyes were unrecognizable, and Nyx couldn't help but focus on them.

"That be the 'Eye' Can," Randolph said. "That was left by me predecessor, Mrs. Richter."

Each set of eyes were meticulously cut and perfectly placed into position on the can. It had not been a five minute slop job. Mrs. Richter had gone into painstaking detail for this memento. Nyx had never met her, but he was surprised someone who had obviously put this much work into a project would just leave it behind.

"Yer brother was a great help t'me today, Mr. Grimm," said Randolph. "I be still figurin' the computer system out."

Randolph had been hired after Mrs. Richter's surprise resignation just prior to the start of school. He was even newer to the district than Nyx was.

"Nigel is the best person I know working with a computer," Nyx said.

Reaching into a small mini-fridge behind his desk, Randolph pulled out bottled water. Cracking the lid, Randolph looked to Nyx, "Would ya like some water?"

"No," Nyx said, still admiring the 'eye' can.

Taking a deep gulp of the water, Randolph sighed heavily in enjoyment.

"That be good. So Mr. Grimm, how did the rest of the day treat ya?"

"Fine."

"No more dazes."

"No."

"Excellent. Have ye adjusted to Parker's Point High?"

"Yes."

Nyx was not in the mood for small talk.

"Good. Are ye likin' yer teachers?" Randolph asked.

"Mr. Randolph, why am I here?" Nyx said, hoping to cut through the baloney.

"Right to the point? Aye. Good fer ye," Randolph said, though Nyx noticed that despite saying he liked it, Randolph had actually not gotten to the point yet.

"So the point is…?" Nyx asked.

"Ye and Mr. Oswald were friends, aye?" Randolph said.

"Yes," Nyx said, adding, "and then he kidnapped and threatened my brother."

"Aye, that he did." Randolph said, looking chapfallen. "In me short time with the boy, I found that Mr. Oswald has impulse control issues."

Ya think? thought Nyx.

"And not to make excuses for him," Randolph said, as Nyx sensed an excuse forthcoming, "but he had been enchanted by the fair lass, Penny Harris. And which o'us have not done foolhardy things in the name of love?"

"Foolhardy? Don't you mean criminal?" Nyx said.

"Semantics," he said.

Semantics? Is he serious? Nyx thought.

"Okay," Nyx said.

"Mr. Oswald has deep seated feelings of betrayal. He has two ultimately successful parents who placed their careers ahead of him. These wounds be runnin' deep," Randolph said.

"Yeah," Nyx said. He had seen that with his own eyes.

"In Julian's eyes, you were one more person to desert him," Randolph said.

"I get it," Nyx said. He did get that.

"I believe Mr. Oswald would be open to a reunion between the two of ya… if ye be willin'," Randolph said.

Nyx didn't know what to say.

"Now, before you say anything…" started Randolph.

"Wait," Nyx interrupted, "I get that Julian felt that I betrayed him when I figured out that he had framed Noah, but that doesn't excuse what he did. He stole money from the football team to frame Noah, because he wanted Noah's girlfriend. And when I found out, he kidnapped Westley and threatened to hurt him if I did not do what he wanted."

"Aye, he did all that."

"Am I supposed to forget that?" asked Nigel.

"Nah, ye're supposed to be forgivin' all that," he said. "Lots o' people have made mistakes. Weren't ye arrested for breakin' and enterin'? The Dietz residence, aye?"

I didn't know he knew that, Nyx thought.

"Um… yeah," Nyx said.

"And ye were forgiven for that, weren't ya?" Randolph asked.

Nyx nodded though he didn't like the way this was trending.

"In fact, the bloke whose house ye broke into is now a friend o' yers, right?" Randolph continued.

"More or less," Nyx said. Nyx was friendly with Shane Dietz, but it was a stretch to call them friends.

"So why doesn't Julian, yer best friend, deserve the same consideration?" he questioned.

"Julian doesn't want to be my friend anymore," Nyx said.

"He is upset. As I said, he feels deserted. Betrayed," Randolph said, "but I think I can convince him to let go of his negative emotions. Deep down… he is still your friend."

Nyx considered what Randolph said. Julian and Nyx had been best friends. *Can I ever fully trust him again,* Nyx thought.

After weighing his options, Nyx said, "I can't promise anything, but I'll try to keep an open mind and see where that takes us. I don't know if Westley will ever be comfortable around Julian ever again."

"Fair enough," Randolph said. "An open mind. That be all I ask."

The antennae shaped scars near Mr. Randolph's temples burned, but he refused to touch them. There was nothing he could do about it anyway. The searing pain had begun to become worse. Time was short.

He stood up and extended his hand toward Nyx. He shook his hand, but Nyx's curiosity was getting the better of him.

"How did you get those scars on your head?" Nyx inquired.

"They are birthmarks," he said, but Nyx didn't believe him. They clearly were scars of some kind, but Nyx didn't press. If it was important enough to lie about, Nyx didn't know how far Randolph might take it to protect the secret. Had Max not told him about Randolph's past, Nyx wouldn't have given a second thought to the story Randolph was spinning. Still, Nyx felt confident to push on.

"I've never met someone working at a school that had an eyebrow piercing. You really are against the grain, aren't you, sir?" said Nyx. "Did Mr. Stanton ask you about it?"

Nyx knew that Mr. Stanton was a straight-laced individual and as assistant principal, he would have had something to say about the hiring of Randolph.

"No, Mr. Grimm," said Randolph, "nobody ever asked me about it. I be guessin' that me skills shined through. And aye, I am an unconventional staffer, and I wouldn't have it any other way."

If he didn't know better, Nyx would almost admire the way Mr. Randolph was his own man no matter what anyone may think about it.

Almost.

Chapter Four

A Warning

"I have seen the writing on the wall.

Don't think I need anything at all."

Pink Floyd

<u>The Wall</u>

The Grimm family home

Westley and Nigel's room

Monday, 4:15 PM

Overrun by the darkspawn, the populace of the city of Denerim within the kingdom of Ferelden shivered in expectation by the continuing invasion by the demonic forces from beneath the surface of Thedas. The powerful archdemon, a being hosted in the body of a massive dragon, threatened life as it was known, and even King Cailan, son of the legendary King Maric, knew not what could be done to prevent the darkspawn's fifth blight.

However, a small, ragtag group of Grey Wardens, the order of heroes entrusted to drive the darkspawn back, united behind the mage shapeshifter named Westley. Westley knew that only one imbued with the Taint, the blood of the darkspawn, could hope to defeat the deadly archdemon. The Taint, however, would as well signify the doom for the hero as well. This conundrum for the mage was exacerbated after an unexpected offer of Morrigan to sire a demigod to battle the dragon. The fate of Ferelden rested in Westley's hands, and the great responsibility of great power weighed upon him.

As Westley stared, unblinkingly, at the screen, the haunting notes of Aubrey Ashburn's award-winning "I Am the One" bombarded his hearing through the headphones. The slight hum of his X Box 360 was inaudible to him as the life and death decisions of *Dragon Age: Origin* completely consumed his imagination. He had been working on this video game since before they moved to Parker's Point, and Westley had invested hours to get to the point he was now at, and those decisions were vital.

Fantasy role-play was easy. Even a poor choice did not signal the end of the game but merely a setback to be fixed by repetition. Westley was finding real life to be much more challenging… with his fears and obsessions not as easily removed with a simple reset.

With the soundtrack blaring over his iPod, Westley was engrossed in the game, chasing away his problems for a short time. Seconds after deciding to take the Taint upon himself and see what happened, a muffled sound distracted him for a brief second. A half-hearted look toward his closed room door confirmed that he was still alone in the room, and Westley returned to the fantasy.

With Westley's senses monopolized by *Dragon's Age* and the music, the young boy did not realize that Nyx had busted through the door and was heading directly toward him. Nyx's face was pale, twisted with a phobic emptiness as his belly tightened with cold, sick fear. Nyx stood in front of his brother, blocking his view.

"Hey!" Westley exclaimed, unhappy with his older brother's rude interruption.

Nyx pulled the headphones from Westley's head, throwing them on the bed beside him.

"Didn't you hear me yelling for you?" Nyx said, his tone shaking Westley more than his words. Placing each hand on his brother's shoulders, Nyx added, "Are you alright?"

"Yeah… why?" Westley asked. A sudden burst of coldness nipped at Westley. He didn't understand why Nyx was so panicked.

"You don't know?" Nyx said, surprised.

"What are you talking about, Nyx?" Westley said, now really uncomfortable.

How is it possible that he doesn't know? Nyx thought.

"How long have you been playing this game?" asked Nyx.

"Since Mom brought me back from school. Why?" asked Westley again.

"Follow me," Nyx said, heading out from the bedroom.

The twins' room was directly across from their parents' room, and a short hallway led from these rooms into the living room. Taking his arm, Nyx pulled his brother along until they reached the family area.

Westley was not prepared for what was revealed.

"Oh my stars and garters," Westley said, his favorite catchphrase spoken by the Beast from the X-Men.

The living room had been wrecked. Tables and chairs were overturned. Shredded paper was scattered around the room. Their mom's ceramic figurines that had decorated the room as long as the boys could remember had been shattered, and broken glass was everywhere. The cushions on the couch had been sliced open and the stuffing within ripped out.

Then Westley's attention was drawn to the living room wall where the Grimm family portrait had once hung. The blue spray paint barely dry, the graffiti delivered a message as confusing as it was frightening:

PSYBOLT UNLEASHED

Westley looked to Nyx, who had calmed down dramatically since his frantic entry into Westley's room. The safety of his brother had eased his worries for now.

"Psybolt?" Westley asked. "Nyx… wasn't that your *Capes and Cowls* character?"

Nyx nodded. He hadn't played the super hero role-playing game *Capes and Cowls* since the problem with Julian. Julian was the GM of those games in the backroom of Bright's Comix, and no one had stepped up to replace him. In fact, Nyx wasn't sure he wanted anyone to do so. Nyx had played Psybolt, and Julian had suggested having Psybolt turn villain on the rest of the group. Nyx didn't want to do this, and, in retrospect, the irony was more than Nyx could handle.

"We need to call Dad," Nyx said.

Soon, the screaming siren and flashing red and blue lights pulled into the Grimm's driveway as Richard Grimm responded to his son's alarmed call. Officer John Dodge had accompanied Richard just in case there was an unavoidable conflict of interest.

"Dad!" Nyx shouted, as Richard entered the room. Disbelief and amazement at the chaotic scene before him pried at his soul. Things like this weren't supposed to happen in Parker's Point.

"Are you boys all right?" asked Richard, as two of his sons rushed over to him. "Where are Nigel and Ariel?"

"Ariel's at gymnastics, and Nigel is there with her," Nyx replied. Richard is able to exhale for the first time since he received the phone call from Nyx.

"Have you called Mom?" he asked.

"I tried. I got her voice mail. Nigel's too," Nyx said.

"Are you okay, Westley?" Richard asked, noticing Westley's restrained demeanor.

"Yes," he said, though not overly convincingly.

"Dad," Nyx whispered, "Westley was here when this was happening."

After hearing the explanation of Westley's sensory deprivation via *Dragon's Age* and its soundtrack, Richard took his son in his arms, holding him tightly but in a comforting embrace.

"I'm so sorry, son," he said, tenderly.

Officer Dodge's deep voice ceased the sentimental moment as the dark skinned officer reached into his pocket to pull out his notebook.

31

"What does 'Psybolt Unleashed' mean?" he asked, writing details into his pocket notebook.

Richard immediately witnessed the exchange of his sons' knowing glances.

"Do you know what this 'Psybolt' is?" he asked.

"Yes," said Nyx, "it was the name of my super hero character. The one I played at Bright's Comix."

"That was with Julian," he said. Richard's eyes closed in realization. He moved over to Officer Dodge. "Julian Oswald did this."

"The mayor's kid? Are you joking, man?" Dodge replied.

"He kidnapped Westley and tried to blackmail Nyx, and he has a grudge against my sons. He is the prime suspect as far as I am concerned."

"Yeah! We thwarted his evil plan," said Westley, finally sounding like himself.

"And he did know about Psybolt," Nyx said. *Things don't look good for Julian. So much for Mr. Randolph's truce,* Nyx thought.

"Nyx, when was the last time you saw Julian today?" Richard asked.

"This morning before school," Nyx answered. "He was acting messed up. And…"

Nyx stopped, not sure if he should mention it.

"What?" his dad said.

"Mr. Randolph asked to see me after school. He wanted me to give Julian another chance. He wanted me to forgive him."

Richard had that "I know exactly what happened" look that Nyx had seen so many times. Richard Grimm was a good police officer, and Nyx knew, from past experience, that fooling him was a difficult task.

Nyx immediately thought back to the Prophesight warning of danger by the vision this morning in science. Nyx had a terrible feeling that this was just the beginning.

Richard and Officer Dodge began their investigation as Nyx sat at the table, and Westley returned to his room. Richard photographed everything in the living room crime scene while Dodge went to look for the point of entry. Nyx was running possible scenarios through his head as he watched his father work. The one thing that he could not shake… whoever had done this, the reference to Psybolt on the wall meant this was a warning for Nyx.

Officer Dodge came back into the living room and said, "I can't find any clear point of entry. No signs of a break in, at least."

"Westley was here," Richard said. "Front door was probably unlocked."

"I'll see what prints I can pull off the front door. Why don't you talk to your neighbors? Maybe somebody saw someone coming inside," said Dodge.

As Officer Dodge was finishing his statement, the door opened and footsteps could be heard in the kitchen.

"What's going on here?"

Billie Grimm was home. She had Nigel and Ariel, and they had been surprised to see the flashing lights of the police car in the driveway. It was not uncommon for the police car to be parked in the driveway of the Grimm residence, but it had never been 'on-duty' before. Billie was concerned.

Walking into the living room, Billie froze. Her eyes expanded as she took in the spectacle.

"Cool! What happened?" Nigel said as he and his little sister followed behind their mother.

"Nigel... go to your room," Billie said, coldly. Looking to Nyx, she added, "Go with him and take Ariel as well."

"Mom!" griped Nigel, but Nyx could tell by the tone of the voice that she meant business.

"Now Nigel!" she said, clearly, with great purpose, her hand resting on her pregnant paunch.

"Yes, Mom," Nyx said, directing his pouting brother and little sister toward the twins' room.

Westley was flopped, stomach first, on his bed staring blankly at the video game. Nigel leaped on his bed and excitedly looked to Nyx. Nigel remembered his conversation with Nyx outside of the guidance office, and he nearly blurted it out, but he was able to curtail the impulse when he saw Ariel spinning around like a top.

"You should have seen me today, Nyx," proudly stated Ariel, oblivious to what had happened in the living room. "We did all kinds of cool stuff, and I was great, wasn't I, Nigel?"

"Yeah, she was good," Nigel said, less enthusiastically.

Nyx believed it. Of the four of them, Ariel easily had the most natural athletic ability, and she was as graceful as a snowflake.

"The teacher said I was the best in the class. I can't wait to go back," she said, continuing to spin around in the cramped room. There had been more space in the room when the twins had their beds stacked in bunk beds, but they had decided to change it up.

"What happened out there?" Nigel said, unable to curb his nature any longer.

"I don't know," Nyx said. "It was like that when I got home."

"Westley?" Nigel asked.

"I was on *Dragon's Age*," he said. His brother knew what that had meant.

"So there was about an hour when this could have happened," Nyx said. "And whoever it was, probably thought you two were at chess club."

"Could it have been someone who knew you were going to Mr. Randolph's office?" asked Nigel.

"You went to Mr. Randolph's office?" asked Westley.

But before the brothers could continue their speculation, Billie knocked on the door, entering without waiting for a response.

"Kids, pack some clothes… we're going to a hotel tonight," Billie said through a clamped jaw. Ariel gave a cheer, but the boys were anything but happy. "Hurry up now."

The sharpness of the tone was unfamiliar territory for Billie, and the reverberation within those few words she spoke said more than she could imagine. As Billie turned away from her children, a jittering swept across her hands so slightly that a stranger would never have perceived it. Nyx was no stranger.

"We'll be leaving in twenty minutes," she said, her normally long majestic neck slouched down between her shoulders. She reminded Nyx of a beaten dog that shied away from sudden movements.

Billie Grimm was a popular author whose *Jacob Horror* series had been developing a loyal following. She always carried herself with grace and dignity and music in her movement, but it seemed as if the music had stopped.

Nyx's room was in the basement so he walked through the living room. Richard and Billie were in Ariel's room, and he could hear them arguing. Officer Dodge was nowhere to be seen. Nyx stopped and looked at the living room's hectic display once more. Reaching down, Nyx grabbed a handful of the shredded paper and shoved it in his pocket.

Two miles west of Parker's Point

Best Western Hotel Lobby

Monday, 6:45 PM

The boys sat in the plush chairs staring at the pool area that, unfortunately, was closed for maintenance. The pool was the only selling point for the boys, and with it gone, the hotel's appeal was at zero for the Brothers Geek.

The plan was to get adjoining rooms with Nyx, Nigel and Westley sharing one, and Billie and Ariel in the other. When they had left home, Richard said he would be staying and not joining them at the hotel. Nyx had considered asking to stay at home with his dad, but there was something fragile about his mom, and he didn't want to upset her further.

Within the next half hour, the boys walked into their hotel room. The smoky dreg vilely perfumed the room's décor.

"Whoa," said Nigel as the stench smacked him on the face like the radiating heat from a furnace. "This room stinks!"

The smoky odor blanketed the room, and Nyx tried not to think about the bed and what might be the plight of the sheets and whatever lived beneath them.

Westley seemed less bothered by the aroma or the potential grossness of the room as he plopped down on the green swivel chair and immediately clicked on the television with the remote. Finding a marathon of *Sliders*, Westley settled in with excitement. Nigel sat on one of the two beds in the room. He wasn't too pleased.

"Can't we find something better?" Nigel complained.

"You're kidding, Nigel?" said Westley. "This rocks!"

"Not these episodes. When they killed off Professor Arturo, the show jumped the shark."

"Arturo was cool. You know, he was Gimli in the *Lord of the Rings*," said Westley.

"Yeah, and Sallah in the Indiana Jones movies," said Nigel.

"He's great," said Westley.

"Yeah he is!" agreed Nigel.

Nyx almost fell down when the twins were agreeing on something.

He looked closely at both of them to make sure they hadn't been replaced by aliens or something.

"We can watch *Sliders* anytime," said Nyx, "but I need to talk to you two, and this is the perfect opportunity. I mentioned this to Nigel earlier today, but I didn't have time to expand. I had another vision with the Prophesight."

"What?" Westley asked.

"Yes," Nyx said, "and I think that the break in at home has to do with what I saw. There was a white skinned man who appeared to me in science class, and he told me... well, he didn't tell me... he insinuated that I was in danger."

"Insinuated?" asked Nigel.

"Yeah, the vision didn't speak to me. He mouthed the word danger and pointed at me. I got the impression that he was unable to talk," Nyx said.

"Can't these visions ever be more specific?" asked Westley. "What danger?"

"I don't know," said Nyx, "but I think if we can identify the man, we can maybe get an idea. I'm going to go see Max tomorrow and find out if he can discover the identity of this man."

"Do you think he was a real person?" asked Nigel. "That's a bit of a stretch, isn't it?"

"Well, maybe... but what else can we do? Last time, the Prophesight spoke through Max, and this time it appeared as this albino. That has to be of some significance. Of course I believe that this danger has some connection to the person who vandalized our house," said Nyx.

"That had to be Julian, didn't it?" asked Westley. "I mean... how many people knew who Psybolt was AND had problems with you?"

"Maybe," said Nyx, not sure that he was convinced. Nyx reached into his pocket and pulled out the shredded paper he had picked up earlier.

"What's that?" Nigel asked.

"Some of the paper from the floor. I didn't know why it was there. It didn't seem to fit with the rest of the destruction so I wanted to take a closer look."

"That's not possible," said Westley. "It's been shredded."

"Yeah, but I was hoping to get an idea of what it was," Nyx said, "and see if it had any importance."

Nyx knew that he was grabbing at straws, but he didn't know what else to do. He would see Max after school tomorrow, but until then, there was nothing to do but speculate. If the paper could help him do that, then maybe he wouldn't feel as helpless as he did.

Placing each strip of paper carefully on the bed, Nyx straightened them and tried piecing them together like the world's hardest jigsaw puzzle that was missing some important pieces. The twins attempted to help, but the enormity of the situation was galling. Nyx had grabbed a handful, but it was, in actuality, a small piece of the overall pie. Nyx realized immediately that putting it back together was a hopeless chore so he took the paper and put it back into his pocket.

Stretching out on the bed, Nyx ran the possibilities through his head. The amount of paper that he had grabbed was just a small sampling of what was there so the shredding had taken some time. *Did the perp bring it with him?* Nyx wondered. *Or was it a matter of opportunity?*

An argument over Jerry O'Connell showed the twins' attention span had been surpassed as Nyx continued his internal monologue. After school tomorrow he planned on heading to Bright's Comix. Max would provide clarification and direction.

But Nyx could not get the images of that white-skinned man from his vision and the blue paint sprayed upon their living room wall out of his head.

Psybolt unleashed?

Chapter Five

Ladies Choice

"We saved the world. I say we party."

Buffy Summers
Buffy, the Vampire Slayer
"Prophecy Girl"

Best Western Hotel

Billie Grimm's Room

Tuesday, 7:15 AM

"I will pick you up after school tonight," said Billie Grimm, "so wait for me right by the office."

Those words deflated Nyx, who had finally drifted to sleep last night after running over the questions he had for Max.

"Mom, it's Tuesday. I'm going to Bright's tonight," said Nyx. Billie knew that Tuesdays were new comic day, though that was only one intended reason for the trip.

"Hm, I think you can miss one Tuesday, Nyx," she said. "It's not like the Spider-man comic won't be there next week."

Nigel and Westley's faces drop and their jaws nearly unhinge at their mother's callous comments. It was clear to both of the twins that their mother didn't know what she was talking about. Simultaneously, Westley and Nigel crossed their arms in front of their chest and their lips disappeared like characters from Japanese Animae.

"But Mom," Nyx said, hoping to convince her to change her mind.

"No buts, Nyx. I will pick you up," she said.

"Why am **I** being punished?" Nyx said, pouting.

"You're not being punished," she said, quietly.

"Sure feels like it. I haven't done anything wrong, but now I'm not allowed to go to the comic shop," Nyx continued.

"I just want you to be safe," Billie said, fighting her emotions and trying to remain strong and stoic in front of the boys.

"Safe from what?" Nyx asked. That was one of the questions he planned on posing to Max.

"Someone broke into our house and violated the sanctity of our home. We don't know what they wanted or why they did it," their mom said, desperately trying to keep her voice steady.

"Mom, that's not fair! We can't just stop living," Nyx said.

"Of course not, but…" Billie stopped. She wasn't sure how to put it into words so her oldest son would understand.

A tap came on the hotel room door, and Richard came inside. The kids greeted their father warmly as he entered. Nyx didn't want to miss the opportunity.

"Dad, Mom won't let me go to Bright's tonight?" Nyx narked. "And I didn't do anything."

"Why not? This is new comic day, isn't it?" Richard said.

"Richard!" Billie said, annoyed that he didn't just support her decision automatically.

"What, Billie? Why can't he go?" Richard asked, but he was cognizant of his wife's emotional state and probable reason for that decision. "Sweetheart, we can't live in fear."

Billie turned away from him, hands on hips. The tension punctured the atmosphere so acutely that even Ariel could tell something was amiss.

"Should we keep the kids home from school? It's probably more dangerous there than anywhere else," Richard said, continuing to press his wife.

With Mr. Randolph there, Dad is more than likely right, Nyx thought.

"Don't be ridiculous," she snapped, the venom spitting from her tongue.

Nyx, witnessing the sudden hostility displayed by his mom, wished he hadn't pitted them against each other. Nyx was just about to tell his dad to forget it and that he'd come home after school when Billie turned on him like a cat pouncing on a mouse.

"Fine, Nyx," she said, "you can go to the comic shop, but you will call me on your cell before you leave school, and then when you arrive at Bright's. And you call before you leave. Do you understand?"

"Yes, Mom. Thanks," Nyx said, apprehensively and full of guilt.

Richard tried to put his arm over her shoulder in a show of support and comfort, but she pushed it away and sat down in the hotel chair.

Resigned, Richard said, "I came over to let you know, Nyx, that Julian was not the one who wrecked the living room."

"What?" Nyx said, not expecting that.

"He has an alibi, and it checked out. Julian Oswald did not commit the vandalism at our house," Richard said. "I wanted you to know before you went to school. That way, you don't have to wonder about him if you see him in the hall."

"Thanks," Nyx said, though it did not make him feel too much better.

At least Julian was the enemy he knew, thought Nyx. *Not knowing was **not** better.*

Billie insisted on driving the kids to school, and after the morning's previous drama, none of them objected. Nyx tried to expunge his parents' turmoil from his thoughts by focusing on the break-in. Questions floated in and out of his internal deliberation.

Who else knew about Psybolt?

Why would anyone want to wreck our living room?

Could it have been someone else from Julian's gaming group?

What did the message 'Psybolt unleashed' mean?

What were they trying to say?

Did they know our schedule, and if so, what does that say about opportunity?

What was the shredded paper left on the floor? Was it significant or just a red herring?

Nyx hoped that Max would be able to provide him with something to go on.

Parker's Point High School

Mr. Schmidt's American Literature

Tuesday, 12:50 PM

"Und ven he had lived long, und vas born to his grave dey carved no hopeful verse upon his tombstone, for his dying hour vas gloom."

Mr. Hans Schmidt taught American literature at Parker's Point High School. The irony of a native German teaching American lit was not lost on the students.

"Achtung, class, vat does Herr Hawthorne mean vith dat final line?" he asked. "Vat does Goodman Brown believe at de end of de story?"

Mr. Schmidt stood at the board, dabbed his sweaty bald head with a handkerchief, and waited for an answer from the quiet horde. The classroom was filled with either blank stares or eyes averting from Mr. Schmidt's glances.

Finally, Nyx raised his hand, dreading the awkward silence eclipsing the class.

"Ja, Herr Grimm," said Mr. Schmidt, sitting his tired old bones down in his teacher's chair.

"Goodman Brown's life is never the same when he discovers his friends and family fall victim to the darkness, and it changes him for the rest of his life," Nyx answered.

"Ja, good Herr Grimm," said Mr. Schmidt, "and…"

"Please excuse this interruption," Principal Kendrick's voice boomed over the recently replaced intercom system. During the first few weeks of school, the intercom would cut out in the middle of announcements. It had become such a source of annoyance for Mrs. Kendrick, she insisted on the replacement of the system. The last week it had worked well… almost too well… as the volume thundered across it.

Mr. Schmidt, irritated at the interruption, tilted back in the chair and mumbled something in German.

"Students of Parker's Point High, I am pleased to announce that this Saturday night, the student council will be sponsoring a …"

The familiar click of the intercom once again cut off the announcements in a strategically important section. The class laughed.

"… this damn thing isn't working," the principal's voice said, booming once again. "Oh, I'm back on? Sor…"

The intercom stopped working for a second time bringing the class to uproarious laughter. Just the thought of Mrs. Kendrick, straight laced and respected principal, stomping and swearing in the office at the newly "fixed" intercom system filled the room with joyous laughter even reducing some to tears. Even Mr. Schmidt suppressed a snicker.

Finally, the intercom came back on.

"I'm sorry," Mrs. Kendrick said, rushing. "I'm going to make this quick. I don't know how long this will last. Saturday night. Student council. Sadie Hawkins Dance. Starts at six. I will e-mail details to the teachers."

"What's a Sadie Hawkins Dance?" asked Bryan Simon.

"A Sadie Hawkins Dance is a dance vere da girls invite de boys," Mr. Schmidt answered, rubbing his wrinkled hands.

The buzz through the room was not going to be stopped by Nathaniel Hawthorne. Nyx wasn't as thrilled as his classmates at the prospect. He had never been popular with the girls. Smallish, glasses, considered a geek, his presumption was that no invite would be in the cards for him. Nyx would avoid the embarrassment of a school dance like the plague.

I probably have things to do anyway, Nyx thought.

Parker's Point High School

The hallway by the twins' lockers

Tuesday, 3:05 PM

Nyx stood in the hall waiting for his brothers to arrive. The afternoon had passed uncommonly quickly, and he was getting ready to head out to Bright's Comix. First, though, he had some business to finish.

"Hi Mom," said Nyx into his phone. "I'm just about ready to head over to Bright's Comix. As soon as the twins get here, I'm heading out."

He would not let himself forget his mother's stern condition for allowing him to go to Max's. He had been reminding himself all day long because he would hate to see her if he had forgotten. Something was weird about the way she had responded to this entire situation. It wasunlike her, and Nyx had seen enough of her pain from this morning. He had tried to put the image of his parents fighting out of his mind, but it was nigh impossible.

"Forget it, it's not gonna happen," said Nigel as the twins approached their lockers.

"Mom, the twins are here," he said, promising to be extremely careful and to be on the watch out for any strangers around. "We'll be fine. Bye."

Billie had insisted that the three of them stay together on their trip to the shop, saying that there would be strength in numbers. That was okay for Nyx as it would give them a chance to discuss the situation on the trip.

"Come on Nigel, when do I ever ask you for anything?" Westley asked.

"All the time! Every single day! Not this time though… you ask for too much," said Nigel.

"What's going on?" Nyx asked, putting his cell phone back in his pocket.

"Westley wants me to go to the dance with Jenette," Nigel said.

"What?" Nyx responded.

"Novella asked me to go to the Sadie Hawkins Dance, but she said she could only go if Jenette went too. So she asked if Nigel would take her," said Westley.

"And Nigel doesn't want to," said Nigel, finishing his brothers statement.

Nyx smiled. He could tell that Westley wanted to go, apparently putting aside his shyness and his sensitivity toward Novella being referred to as his "girlfriend."

"No," said Nigel.

"Come on, brother," said Westley.

"No."

"Nyx," said Westley, hoping that his older brother could help him convince his stubborn twin that this would not be the worst thing in the world.

"Sorry, Westley," Nyx replied. "If Nigel doesn't want to go, he doesn't have to. You can't force him."

Westley was disappointed, but he was determined that this was not over.

"Did you call Mom?" Nigel asked, surprising Nyx with his sudden responsibility.

"Yep. It's all taken care of," Nyx said, "so as soon as you guys are ready, we can head to Bright's."

The Brothers Geek began their voyage from the school to one of the places where they felt at home. Nyx tried not to let the fact that his younger brother had an invite from a girl for the Sadie Hawkins dance and that his other younger brother was turning down a date bother him, though it was a tad emasculating. Nyx tried to pinpoint the thread to maximize his brothers' attention spans.

"Did either of you guys see Julian today?" asked Nyx.

"I didn't," said Westley.

"Nope," replied Nigel.

"I didn't either," Nyx said. "I wonder if he was not here today. That seems kind of coincidental that he was gone the day after our home was vandalized."

"You heard Dad, Nyx," said Nigel. "It couldn't have been Julian. He had an air tight alibi."

"Yeah, I just have a feeling that he is involved in this somehow. Maybe he didn't actually perform the task, but he has got to be involved. Who else knew about Psybolt that would hold a grudge with us?"

"With us?" Westley asked.

"Hey," Nyx said, "we are the Brothers Geek, right?"

Nyx had been pulling that line out more and more. He knew that the twins identified with the nickname, and it would be an easy way to keep them doing things that he wanted. Nyx knew it was a little manipulative. He was okay with that.

"Fine… with us," Nigel said, acquiescing.

"But would Julian trust someone else to carry out his dirty work?" Westley said.

"Could be," Nyx said. "He tried to get me to do what he wanted. Why not someone else? He has enough money."

"Okay," Nigel said, "so who is his accomplice?"

"Mr. Randolph?" Nyx said.

"Now you're off your rocker," Westley said.

"Why would Mr. Randolph want to vandalize our house?" Nigel said.

"We know he's been involved with one of Max's cases from a few years ago. We know that he was involved in… terrible things," Nyx said, not wanting to think about the atrocities Max claimed Randolph committed. "If that is true, why would vandalism be a stretch?"

"What is his motive?" Westley asked.

"I don't know. Maybe some kind of revenge against Max," Nyx said, though he knew that didn't sound right. In fact, Nyx had been struggling to try and place any kind of motive for Randolph's arrival in Parker's Point. None of this made much sense to the young geek.

"Mr. Randolph hasn't done anything to us since he arrived here," said Westley. "I think you're obsessed with him."

"Maybe you're right," Nyx said, but he knew what he felt. *Randolph was involved too*, Nyx thought, *but how and why?*

The conversation took a sudden change with the interruption of the siren screeching like a banshee. The red fire engine flashed past them, full speed ahead. Nyx had a sinking feeling in the pit of his stomach.

"Come on," he said to his brothers as they all started running in the direction that the fire engine had traveled.

Smoke forming in the air above the building could be seen from the distance, and the estimated distance was about right. Nyx hoped he was wrong.

But he wasn't.

As they came around the corner, they saw the flames shooting from the windows of Bright's Comix. The heat was like a furnace, billowing out from the all-consuming fire. The posters from the windows burned to ashes, and the charred walls weakened and consumed with flame.

Bright's Comix was ablaze.

Chapter Six

Torched

"Now picture that... but everywhere! I mean... everywhere!"

Johnny Storm, the Human Torch
Fantastic Four (2005)

2342 Central Street, Parker's Point

Bright's Comix

Tuesday, 3:35 PM

Nyx couldn't believe his eyes. The orange and red danced out the window, combusting oxygen and scorching the walls and ceiling of the comic shop. The thought of the loss of all those back issues was almost too much for them to bear.

"Ook Ook now fire," said Nigel, somewhat callously quoting a comedy song in the middle of this tragedy. Nyx glared at his brother before the flashing realization struck him.

"Where's Max!" Nyx blurted out, scanning the crowd for any sign of the owner of the blazing structure.

"He's okay," Westley said, reassuringly, but not convincingly.

Nyx thought about the injured leg that had hindered Max for the last five years. The possibility that the leg had prevented an escape from the inferno scared him.

"He's fine," Nigel said. "He's in that organization of secret agents. Those kinds of people don't just burn up in buildings."

In reality, Max was more than just a comic shop owner. That was a cover. He was a member of a secret society called the Guild of the Hidden. Truthfully, Nyx was not sure of what Max was capable. Nyx was so worried that he did not even chastise Nigel for his "secret agent" quote.

"Quite the blaze, yes?"

The brothers immediately recognized the false American accent coming from behind them, and they turned happily to see the smiling, slightly singed, Max Bright.

"Hello, gentlemen," Max said, always polite.

"You're ok!" Nyx said, nearly jumping at him.

"That I am, fortunately. My store has seen better days, I'm afraid," he said. "I'm glad to see you three."

"Max, we need to talk," Nyx said.

"Yes, I think that would be in order," Max said, "but I'm afraid that I won't be able to leave here anytime soon."

"Nyx, do you think the same person who did this," Nigel started, pointing at the flames, "wrecked our living room?"

"What does he mean?" Max asked. "Did something else happen?"

"A lot actually," Nyx began, but before he could expand further, Nyx stopped as he spotted his father crossing the street on a beeline for them.

"Guys, is everyone alright?" Richard asked as he arrived.

"We just got here, Dad," Westley said.

"Good. I was worried when I heard the call on the scanner. Mr. Bright, I'm sorry about your store."

"Please sir, call me Max. And thank you for your kind words."

"Okay, Max. I need to get a statement from you," Richard continued, switching gears from concerned parent to police officer.

"Of course," Max said.

As they began to walk away, Richard turned back and said, "You'd better give your mother a call, Nyx. She'll be worried."

"Shoot!" Nyx said. With the excitement of the fire, Nyx had forgotten to call Billie when they arrived. He quickly pulled out his cell phone, frantically pressing the speed dial button.

"Hi, Mom, we're here," Nyx said, debating whether or not to reveal the full truth to his mom. She had been acting so erratic lately.

"What took you so long? I was getting worried!" she said.

"Sorry. I forgot because," Nyx paused a moment to take a deep cleansing breath, "Bright's Comix is on fire."

"Oh my goodness!" she exclaimed. "What happened? Is everyone alright?"

"Yes," Nyx answered. "Max is fine, and the place was already burning when we got here. Dad is here talking to Max, and the fire fighters are trying to put out the fire."

"Good," she said and Nyx wondered if his parents were still fighting. It sounded to Nyx that his mom was relieved that Richard was on scene, but he wasn't sure if he was misreading her signals over the phone.

"Mom, I want to talk to Max before we come home," Nyx said, deciding to press his luck. "Is that alright?"

The long pause on the phone said more than any words could say, and Nyx thought he heard a slight sob through the receiver.

What is going on with her? Nyx thought.

Just as he was about to rescind his request, Billie said, in a soft, uncomfortably sad voice, "Ok, just please be careful and call me when you are starting for home."

50

"We'll be fine, Mom," Nyx said, trying to tenderly reassure her. He could tell she had not been the same since the break-in yesterday, and he was becoming even more concerned about her.

Putting the cell phone back into his jeans pocket, Nyx looked over to Max.

"What did she say?" Nigel asked.

"Was she okay with us staying to talk to Max?" Westley said.

"I'm not sure okay is the right term," said Nyx. "She said we could, though."

After waiting for Max to conclude his statement to their father and his discussions with the fire fighters, the Brothers Geek anxiousness began to show.

"I have some time now to talk," Max said. "But we can't talk about these matters here in the street. Come, follow me."

Leading the boys down around the corner from the blazing debris of Bright's Comix, Max started walking toward an old diner, a neon sign flashing the word Joe's placed squarely in the window. The tacky blue curtains obstructed the 'J' and the 'S' but both shone through the thin material.

Opening the glass door, Max held his arm out, inviting the Grimm boys to enter the diner.

"I know this place doesn't look like much, but they serve a brilliant cup of tea," Max said, letting his hidden British side creep through for a moment.

Once inside, the boys' eyes adjusted to the dim lights and the musty smell of greasy food bombed their olfactory senses. With each step upon the black and white checkerboard floor, Nyx, Westley and Nigel had to maintain their balance in fear of slipping on the slick tile.

"Hey there, Maxie," said a lone voice. A slightly chubby, strawberry blonde waitress exited through the swinging doors from the kitchen area holding a blue order pad. The outfit the women wore matched the curtains hanging over the sign in the window, and Nyx wondered which came first. The woman was clearly unaware of the drama that had engulfed Max's afternoon, and he was not in a rush to reveal it to her. Not at this moment, at least.

"Good afternoon, Tricia," Max said, turning back to the brothers. "Would any of you like a refreshment...soda, perhaps?"

"Yeah!" Nigel said, already hyper.

"Thanks," said Westley, more restrained than Nigel.

Nyx nodded, appreciative of his brothers' enthusiasm and politeness, respectively.

"Dear Tricia, we will be back in the foyer," Max said, with a lilt in his delivery. Max had pointed to a back room area that was split apart from the outer diner. Though not enclosed completely, this would provide them a modicum of privacy for what they had to discuss.

"Sounds good, Hon," she said as her heavily painted eyelid winked at Max. Her bright ruby lips blew him a kiss as her plump cheeks shimmered.

After they settled in the corner booth in the back room, Tricia brought them their sodas along with several donuts to satisfy Max's sweet tooth, and they exchanged barbs,what could only be defined as flirting. The comic book store owner and the waitress shared a comfortableness at which Nyx was surprised. It was sweet, but Nyx had never pictured Max in this way.

"If there's anything else you boys need, just give me a holler," said Tricia, tucking the order pad into the white apron that wrapped around her ample waist.

"We will, Tricia," said Max, "thank you."

With the waitress on her way back to the kitchen, Max got down to business.

"Now… tell me about your living room," Max said, taking a sip of tea.

"I will, but first you have to know that I had another," Nyx paused, not sure what the correct term for it would be, finally settling on, "bout of Prophesight."

"What?" Max said, placing the tea down on the cracked Linoleum of the corner booth. "Tell me."

"Yes, yesterday morning before science class," he said.

"What message did you receive?" he asked.

"Danger," Nyx replied.

"How very cryptic," said Max.

"Tell me about it, but there's more," continued Nyx. "This wasn't like the last time. This time I saw… someone… in the vision… a man. He had white skin and long white hair with gray eyes. He was weird. He looked very thin… almost like those pictures of the malnourished kids from Africa."

"Interesting. What did he say?" Max beckoned.

"That's the thing. He didn't say anything. In fact, I got the definite impression that he couldn't say anything. He mouthed the word 'danger' and pointed at me. Then he was gone," Nyx said.

"And then our house was wrecked," Nigel said, brushing the donut powder from his face.

Again shocked, Max said, "What?"

"Yeah," Nyx said. "When I got home from school yesterday, the living room had been trashed."

"I was home playing a video game in my room," Westley said.

"Good lord, are you all, alright?" a concerned Max said, taking Westley by the hand. Max had been wondering why Westley was not quite himself.

"Yes, I'm fine," he said, slowly.

"Someone tore up the room and wrote the words 'Psybolt Unleashed' on the wall in blue spray paint," Nyx finished.

"Psybolt? Why does that sound familiar to me?" Max asked, searching his memory for the uncommon name.

"That was the name of my *Capes & Cowls* character in Julian's Friday night campaigns we'd play in your backroom," Nyx responded.

"Ah… of course, that's it. Bollocks! Could your Uber Geek be at it again?" Max said, jumping to the same assumption that the Grimm family did.

"That's what we thought, but Dad said that Julian had an alibi. He didn't do it," Nigel said.

"So yesterday your house is broken into and vandalized, and today my shop is burned down. Surely that is not a coincidence," Max deduced.

"That's my thought, too," Nyx said. "What happened?"

"Well," Max started, "I was working in the backroom cleaning when I heard a crash… the sound of broken glass. By the time I came up front, the store was ablaze."

"So someone threw something through your window and started the fire?" Westley asked.

"That's what it looked like," Max answered. "The comics went up like kindling."

"Oh! Don't say that!" Nigel said, mourning.

"Sorry," said Max.

"So this 'danger' vision is our only real clue. I was hoping that you could find out something… anything about this white skinned omen. Maybe he was a real person."

"Yes, I'll see what I can find. Actually…" Max stopped speaking, and he had a faraway look cross his face.

"Max?" said Nyx.

"Nyx, let me ask you. This 'Psybolt' character of yours that you played, what kind of powers did he have?" questioned Max as if he already knew the answer.

"He was a mentalist," Nyx responded.

"I think I know where to start looking," Max said. "I'll… let you know what I discover."

Midway through the sentence, Max had dropped his real British accent and continued speaking in his fake American one. That was strange, but Nyx and his brothers didn't ask him about it. Max's demeanor changed dramatically as well. He had become guarded and reserved as he slowly sipped the tea. His eyes darted around the room in a way that was nearly imperceptible. Nyx, however, had seen it.

"What's going on, Max?" Nyx asked, but the question was met with a slight head shake.

"So, how are things going for you, gentlemen, at your school?" Max asked. The subject change was jarring.

"There's a dance this weekend," said Westley, not picking up on Max's subtle clues. "It's a Sadie Hawkins dance."

"Really?" Max said, feigning interest.

"I have an invitation, but only if Nigel goes too, and he's being a jerk about it," Westley said.

"Am not. I just don't want to go," Nigel said.

"Novella won't go unless you go with Jenette," Westley said, unaware of anything else around him. "Why won't you go?"

"I don't want to go," he retorted. "Why do you want to go so badly? Just because of your girlfriend?"

"She's not my girlfriend," Westley said, not answering the question.

As the twins continued their latest inane conversation, Nyx glanced around the greasy spoon to see if he could determine what had altered Max's behavior. There was a man studying the diner's menu as he sat at a table just outside of the back room within earshot of their conversation. Nyx hadn't seen this man sit down, but the stranger's arrival was obviously what had affected Max. Turning back to the comic store owner, Nyx saw Max's eyelids rise ever so cunningly, and his pupils zoomed in the direction of the unknown man hiding behind the menu. It was as if Max was communicating to Nyx without words. Nyx's suspicions were confirmed via Max's crafty facial skullduggery.

Nyx had recognized but not deciphered Max's nonverbal clues, but he had never seen that man before, and he had no idea what, if anything, Max wanted him to do. Nyx knew he had to watch what he said.

With the twins' argument maintaining steam, Nyx had a brainstorm. He normally played moderator between his brothers, but this was an opportunity to try something creative to communicate with Max.

Picking up his soda and pressing the glass against his lips, Nyx did not take a drink. Instead, he whispered a question to Max.

"Who's that guy?"

The liminal inquiry was barely articulate among the constant banter of Nigel and Westley's debate. Max smiled as he was the only person to have heard Nyx's query. He was impressed with the youngster's ingenuity under the circumstances, and he found himself full of pride. Despite the boy's own misgivings and doubt, Max believed Nyx was a natural at this. In truth, Max had seen plenty of others who did not have the instincts of Nyx Grimm, and who washed out under the pressure.

Following the teenager's example, Max lifted his tea cup back to his mouth, and he said, sotto voce...

"I know him."

Chapter Seven

A Ghost from the Past

"The point is... there is always a story. You just have to find it."

Rick Castle
Castle
Flowers for your Grave

Joe's Diner

Just outside the back room

Tuesday, 4:10 PM

Rex Riley took his seat at the diner table, and without hesitation, grabbed the menu to use as a shield. He wasn't sure if the comic book store owner would recognize him, but he didn't want to take the chance. The last time he saw Max Bright, he was sure he was dead. Actually, he was sure they were both dead. He was wrong on both counts.

The waitress brought him a coffee, and she asked if there was anything else he wanted.

"Just the coffee," Rex growled with his dark, bushy eyebrows arched. Tricia got the point and headed back to her station.

Rex didn't know what he was doing here. He was always in the dark. The comic shop owner was drinking tea and entertaining three kids less than an hour after his store burned down. That was strange. Yet, he wanted Bright followed and Rex always followed his instructions. Sometimes Rex wasn't even sure why he did. It was like a compulsion. Whenever he called, Rex came running.

Now he found himself back in America…somewhere called Parker's Point… despite the numerous warrants with his name upon them. This remained a danger.

Rex wondered how much this really had to do with Bright, and how much this had to do with those kids that were with him. He had long ago stopped searching for motive. He rarely understood them anyway.

Rex did not often think of those days past. It was easier not to remember. Not that his conscience bothered him because his conscience**never** bothered him. He had been diagnosed once as a sociopath,which made excuses all the easier. The past was just that, and it could not be changed. Rex was not into wasting time on regret.

When Rex received the unexpected phone call beckoned him to Parker's Point, he really didn't want to come. He had moved on a while ago, but the pull was too strong to overcome. It was always the same. He could never say no to Anthony Randolph.

Glasgow, Scotland

The Pot O'Gold Pub

6 years ago

Rex Riley sat nervously drinking his whiskey. He had responded to a summons from Anthony Randolph. He hadn't seen Randolph since they were kids in Aberdeen. They were close, but the years had been rough on Rex Riley, and the memories of playing with Anthony and Anthony's two younger brothers had sustained him through the ups and the downs. He had left Aberdeen and had become embroiled with horrendous people who committed terrible acts of violence. Rex had not shied away from it, and his reputation preceded him.

It was this reputation that worried Rex. He did not want to appear to be a monster in his childhood friend's eyes, yet how could he not be. He had done so much.

When Anthony walked into the Pot O'Gold, Rex knew right away that something was not right. Randolph's red locks were gone, leaving only a clean, bald head. He was thin, and the aura of sickness that inundated him was unmistakable.

"Anthony!" Rex beckoned with a wave of his hand. His friend of his youth was almost too tired, but he responded with a weak smile.

"Me frein," Randolph said separated by a cough. "Laddie, ye be a bonny sight for me wee eyes."

"Anthony, are you alright?" Rex asked, shocked at what he saw. He remembered Anthony as being full of life. This shell was difficult for Rex to even look at, but he persevered. He could do it for his friend.

"Where be your accent, laddie?" Randolph said. Rex had made a conscious decision to drop the Scottish brogue years ago. It was just one more identifying feature that Rex wanted to avoid.

"You don't look good," Rex said, ignoring the question.

"Aye. Ah be sick. Ah seen me better days," he replied.

"What's wrong?" Rex said.

"Brain tumor," Anthony said as Rex felt the air expel from his lungs.

He hadn't seen him for years, but he considered Anthony a friend. One of the few he had left.

"Dear lord," Rex said.

"It be inoperable," Anthony said, compounding the bad news.

"I'm so sorry," said Rex. "Have you talked to Fletcher and Wallace?"

"Nae. Me brothers… they be dead," Anthony said,

"Good lord. What happened?" a bewildered Rex asked.

"They were… killed… in a… car bomb in Belfast a few years ago," said Anthony, still showing the pain of the loss on his soul. "But this be not about them. This be about me."

"Is there anything I can do to help you?"

"Aye, there jus' may be," Anthony said, a cold grin stretched across his decrepit face and cleared away the good boy image Rex had remembered.

Scottish bluff overlooking the Atlantic Ocean.

Lennox Tower

5 years ago

It had takenMax Bright a good six months to make the connection and track them here. At first, the Guild of the Hidden had assigned Max the task of investigating the use of dark magic in the northern lands of Great Britain. Max, after all, was an expert in all things mystic. It wasn't until recently that he had connected the series of child abductions ravaging families on the island to this case.

His investigation led him to this castle on a bluff with a breathtaking view of the Atlantic. Owned under multiple aliases, Max had determined the true owner was a terrorist named Rex Riley. However, there was no evidence that Riley had ever even dabbled in dark magic, and a novice would not have had such success in hiding what he was doing. This told Max that there was more to this than met the eye.

The cloudless night made cover a challenge as the crescent moon illuminated the dark ocean water creating the sensation of the macabre, and Max could not shake the morbid vibe that tingled from his neck down to his toes. Twinkling stars filled the nighttime sky with the mighty hunter Orion battling the bull for the affection of the seven sisters of the Pleiades... among other stories.

Max saw the portcullis closed across the entrance to the rundown castle. A new padlock adorned the bars and since Max did not have the gate key, he knew he had to find an alternate method of entry. He considered picking the lock, but the castle gate was too much out in the open. There had to be another way.

Eyeing an open window up the tower, Max began slowly scaling the castle wall. Cracks between the bricks and mortar provided tenuous footholds as Max taxed his "mountain climbing" skills to the ultimate level.

After a cautious and deliberate climb, Max pulled himself onto the window ledge. His muscles screamed at him for this decision, but Max had been able to enter unforeseen. The immediate odor of decay told Max what the near future held for him.

Climbing inside, Max tracked the scent to a room inside the tower. Despite his knowledge of the offending odor, Max was unprepared for the abhorrent sight assaulting his eyes. He could not breathe as he took in the horrific scene on display throughout the room. The young bodies, rotted and withered as if drained of their very essence, were discarded like garbage. Their deaths looked painful as the bodies' features were contorted, wrenched into frozen visage of anathema. Even a seasoned professional like Max, who had seen so much tragedy and calamity during his years as part of the Guild of the Hidden, was physically affected by the abomination. Not wanting to further contaminate the scene, Max rushed from the room before the contents of his stomach retraced their original path.

Steadying himself, Max wiped his mouth clean and silently swore an oath to bring the monsters responsible for this carnage to justice. These children would be avenged.

Max continued to search through the castle, unsure what he was looking for, but feeling the need to do something. Each room was both a disappointment and a relief. Max prayed he would find no more innocents within this castle of doom.

A muffled whimper caught his attention, and Max quickly followed the sound. A padlocked door prevented Max's progression as he placed an ear to the wood hoping to determine the origin of the sad sound. The padlock would not present a major obstruction as Max's skills at picking locks were superior. The lock removed, Max threw open the door with no regard for his own personal safety.

Six boys, all between ten and twelve years old, were chained to the wall. The opening of the door initially brought a fearful expression to the children, but with Max's entry a slow, hopeful countenance covered the boys.

Max moved into action quickly. Max chose the boy who appeared to be the oldest of the group, looking at the chain that held the boy in place.

"Hiya. I'm Max. What's your name, son?"

"Brodie," he said, uncertain about the new arrival.

"I'm going to get you lads out of 'ere," he said, starting to work on the chain locks. The memory of the destiny of the others spurred Max on. *These boys would not suffer the same fate*, Max told himself. "What is going on 'ere, Brodie?"

"We were kidnapped. Chained in here by a man," he replied.

"A man? Do you know his name?" said Max, expecting the boy to say Rex.

"He said his name was Anthony," Brodie replied.

"Anthony? What does this Anthony want with you?" Max said, already with a guess in his head. Max wanted to see how much the boy knew about what was going on.

"I don't know," he said. "He said he was sorry for bringing us here, but that he needed us. He never told us for what. And there were others beside us. When he came to take them away, they never came back."

"Was this Anthony the person who kidnapped you?"

"No," Brodie replied. "It was another man. I don't know his name."

The boy described Rex Riley to a tee. So, this Anthony had Rex kidnap the kids and bring them to this castle for some dastardly purpose. *But what?* Max thought.

"Follow me," said Max, after releasing the six lads.

The search for Rex Riley and his accomplice had taken a back seat as Max had assumed the responsibility for these six boys' lives, and he would not take that responsibility lightly. They would not fall victim as the others did… this, Max promised. He didn't care what had to be done; these boys were going to survive.

At ground floor, Max realized that the portcullis was no longer locked, telling him that they were no longer alone.

A harrowing whisper saturated the stale castle air and the boys' tears peppered the stone floor. The boys were not surprised by the soft, hushed tone. It was something they had heard before. But now, so close to freedom, the sound was a cruel twist indeed.

"What the bloody 'ell is that?" Max said, seeing one of the boys freeze in his tracks. Max snatched him and flipped him over his left shoulder. "Double time now, lads."

The whisper increased volume as a thin and pale phantom zoomed from the west past them, causing Max to duck. The spectral kamikaze's volant flight ricocheted from wall to wall within the stone monolith.

Max knew what this malevolent creature was. There was no mistaking either those dark ebony eyes, or the smell of death and decay. The dark hair just added to his confidence. This was a sluagh.

He had seen the sluagh before, though never solo as this one was. They would travel in flocks like birds. Sluagh were evil spirits, seen generally as sinners, who were not welcome in the Otherworld. Legend stated that these creatures attempted to take souls of the dying or the innocent with them, intercepting the soul prior to its reaching Heaven.

However, this was something else. Stories were told throughout Ireland and Scotland about the sluagh kidnapping children, but there had never been any evidence of these crimes. The sluagh was used as a boogyman for parents to modify their children's behavior. *"Be good or the sluagh will get you."*

"Be ready," Max said, leaning over to Brodie and handing him the boy Max was carrying. "When I tell you, run out of here, follow the path back to the town below, and do not look back."

"But," Brodie started.

"No buts, Brodie. I'm counting on you, mate," said Max.

Brodie nodded sadly. He knew what this man had intended to do.

"So we be havin' a guest."

The impeccably dressed Scot stepped into view, and, immediately, the sluagh began zipping around this man like an electron around an atom. An iron cross choker peeked out from behind his light blue ascot.

"An ye be?" he asked. "An' wha' be ye doin' wit' me property?"

"You must be Anthony," Max said, trying to catch him off-guard.

"Aye. Anthony Randolph thae be me ain name. Ye seem t' have me at a disadvantage. Who ar' ye?"

"Max Bright… and these lads are coming with me," he replied. "I'm returning them to their rightful homes."

"A pleasure to meet you Mr. Bright. I have heard many things about you," said Randolph, now trying to shake Max. "However, ah cannae allow thae t'happen. The wee children be mine"

"Bugger that," Max said. "I saw what you intend for these boys, and that is not going to happen. It is unacceptable."

"Ah be havin' no choice," Anthony said, rubbing his scar-free bald head. "Brain tumor. Thae be me treatments."

"What?" a shocked Max said. Then, it all made sense. "So the kids… you have the sluagh… drain their… and you use it to…"

It was such a horrible thought that Max couldn't even put it into words. The vision of those bodies upstairs bombarded him. To know these innocent children were "fed" to this selfish monster… to save his life was a truth too ugly to bear.

"You're a vampire!" Max exclaimed.

"Nae. There be no such thing," Randolph said. "This be Darwin a'his finest. Survival o' the fittest. Ya can be understandin' thae, can ye? Ah only be doin' wha' ah need to survive."

"You're sick," Max said, "and I don't mean with the tumor. This ends tonight."

"Aye, for ya it will," Randolph said, rubbing the iron cross around his neck. Like a projectile, the sluagh launched itself at the boys.

"Run!" Max exclaimed, throwing himself between the sluagh and the boys. Brodie followed Max's directions as the six of them rushed out of the castle without even a second look behind.

The force of the blow from the sluagh drove Max crashing into the gray brick wall. Landing hard with a thud, Max instinctually knew he could not take another shot like that, and he did not have time to recover. Max rolled away from the follow-up attack by the creature. He was not going to be able to keep this up for long, but within his foggy mind, Max had the seed of an idea. An idea that required them to be outside. With blood trickling from his mouth, Max gathered himself and dove for the castle exit.

The cold wind had blown in a mist from the ocean, and the pellets of water falling from the sky helped clear the cobwebs from Max's head. The formerly clear sky filled with dark clouds, an ominous warning as Max moved closer to the edge of the bluff. If his idea was wrong, then he would lead them away from the path of the fleeing children. Max would be the distraction.

Randolph soon followed Max from the castle, but there was no sign of the sluagh.

"I was bloody right!" Max taunted as Anthony Randolph stalked him like a lion on the hunt. "You bound that… thing to yourself, but it can't leave the castle… can it?"

"Aye," Anthony confirmed, "it were too strong. Ah had no choice, but ta bind it to t'castle. But ah dinnae need the sluagh now. Look a'yerself, Mr. Bright. Ye ar' barely standin,' boyo."

Pooling his strength, Max lunged at Randolph. A right cross to the Scotsman's jaw showed that the Brit had something left after all. A knee into Randolph's solar plexus forced exhaled air from his lungs. Max followed this stroke by grabbing Randolph by each shoulder, twisting his own hips, and flipping Randolph over his side. The Scotsman landed hard on the green grass, and Max dropped atop him.

"Anthony!"

The cry from out of nowhere distracted Max for the briefest moment as he looked over to see headlights of a parked car cutting through the darkness, and Rex Riley standing partially out of the car. A look of disbelief was written across his face.

The diversion was long enough for Randolph to drive his hand into Max's throat and roll him over to the ground. Max coughed and hacked, but the oxygen was suddenly cut off. Randolph had both hands wrapped around Max's throat as he locked both elbows and pressed down with as much force as he could muster. Randolph's thumbs dug into Max's gullet as the Scot's teeth buried into his own lip. A tiny drop of blood fell upon Max's cheek as he clawed helplessly at the arms constricting his air. With the light mist falling against his skin, Max's chest burned and his head started to spin. The grip was stronger than he expected. With Riley approaching, Max started to accept the inevitable.

A flash of lightning crossed the dark night momentarily highlighting the situation for Max. A scant glitter was Max's last hope as he grasped the iron cross around Randolph's neck. With whatever strength he could assemble, Max yanked the cross from its place and heaved it backwards. The cross went over the bluff and fell into the dark waters sixty feet below.

"No!" Randolph screamed, releasing his hold and diving toward the edge. Max gasped desperately, as red marks formed upon his neck. "What have ye done?"

The frightening scream of instant freedom from inside the castle was not covered by the rumbling thunder above. Randolph slowly stumbled to his feet and staggered a few feet toward Lennox Tower.

"What's happening, mate?" Rex said, fear taking root in his heart.

Before Anthony could answer his childhood friend, the sluagh came crashing through the closed gate, a runaway locomotive. With the rain now pouring down, the sluagh barreled through Rex, casting him aside like a worthless rag doll. The sluagh knew what it was targeting. It headed directly at Anthony Randolph.

"No… ah command ya," was all Anthony Randolph was able to say as the sluagh slammed into its former master. Randolph's momentum projected him backwards into Max, who had just struggled to his feet. Both men hurled through the air and over the side of the bluff.

Max slowed his descent temporarily by grabbing a root jutting out from the bluff. The maneuver was not going to prevent Max from falling, but it kept him from being thrown way out into the water. Randolph was not as lucky.

Plummeting, Max splashed into the torrent near the bottom of the bluff. Unfortunately, he had not escaped unscathed. As Max hit the water, immediate pain from his leg shot through his body. A hidden rock beneath the waves had stopped Max's fall with devastating and eternal results for his leg.

Fighting to remain conscious with a worthless leg sending waves of agony across him, Max struggled to stay afloat as the rain drummed the water without mercy. Max was grateful that it had been his leg that struck the concealed rock and not his head or back. Not that it mattered now as Max succumbed to the darkness in his head that he had been fighting against.

Let the boys be safe, Max thought before passing out.

The warmth from the morning sun upon his neck awoke Max, returning the pain from his multiple injuries. Max lay face down on the shore beneath the bluff, and he realized that the waves had brought him back instead of out to sea. Gritting his teeth, Max attempted to roll off his stomach. The bone protruding from his leg made that nearly impossible.

"Max, you're alive!"

The female voice belonged to Kate Conway, one of the Guild of the Hidden's top members. Max had become close to her and her husband over the last few years. They had an exceptionally talented son who Max had enjoyed talking to.

"Max, speak to me," Kate said, helping support him.

"At least they didn't send Gwrach," Max said aloud though he had believed that he just thought it. "Kate! There were six boys…"

"They're fine, Max. How do you think we found out where you were?"

"In the castle…" Max weakly said.

"We know. We found them," she said. "Was this Rex Riley?"

Max, with some help, sat up and looked out over the now calm water.

"No. It was someone else, but he's gone," Max said.

Joe's Diner

Rex Riley's table

Tuesday, 4:21 PM

Rex Riley continued to be amazed that this Brit survived the attack of the sluagh and the fall from the bluff five years ago. Riley had looked over the side after the sluagh left, but he saw nothing except darkness. He was sure they were both gone. He would never have guessed that all three of them would find their way to Parker's Point.

And now, Bright owned a comic book store, entertaining children. Rex was almost disappointed. *How the mighty had fallen*, he thought. *Perhaps Max Bright died that day after all.*

With a tiny snicker, Rex took a sip of his coffee. *How easy this is*, he thought.

Max pulled out his cell phone and began to dial. He had made no move toward Rex, and Rex was sure he had not seen him. His arrogance continued to grow.

"Yes, hello officer. This is Max Bright. I am around the corner at Joe's Diner, and I remembered something of vital importance that I'd like you to know immediately," said Max, loudly.

Max's eyes shot over toward Rex, who nearly choked on his coffee. Their eyes made contact, but Max's face did not betray any knowledge. Max's eyes spoke volumes though. Rex knew.

Max Bright recognized him.

Chapter Eight

An Unexpected Invitation

"Last night, Darth Vader came down from the planet Vulcan and told me that if I didn't take Lorraine out that he'd melt my brain."

George McFly
Back to the Future

Parker's Point High School

Hallway

Wednesday, 11:32 AM

Nyx couldn't believe what he saw. Rex Riley was standing in Mr. Randolph's office doorway, and Rex was obviously agitated. He was keeping his voice down, but his mannerisms and body language made up for the lack of volume. Rex Riley was upset. Mr. Randolph looked as if he was fiercely trying to maintain control like the boy with his finger in the dam who just realized he couldn't stop the water from flowing.

"Remember, I know what you did to Diego... and after he saved your life!" exclaimed Rex, the screamcausing Randolph to wince in embarrassment.

Randolph saw Nyx, and he quickly grabbed Rex and redirected him inside the room away from the prying eyes. Nyx smiled as the door slammed. Max's gambit yesterday at the diner was paying off.

As soon as Max had called the police and made eye contact with him. Rex bolted for the door. He tried to be nonchalant about it, but the concern was difficult for him to shroud.

With Rex gone, Max told the boys who Rex Riley was and how dangerous he was. Max didn't come right out and say it, but Nyx could tell that Max believed Rex was the person responsible for torching the comic shop.

"Rex Riley is an extremely dangerous man, and if you see him again, you should avoid him at all costs," warned Max.

"Do you think he broke into our house and wrecked the living room?" asked Nigel.

"Could be," Max said.

"But... how would Rex Riley know about Psybolt? That is something... that is something that he..." Nyx started, pausing as flickers of memory energized his brain.

"What is it, Nyx?" asked Westley. "Is your Spidey-sense tingling?"

"When I first met Mr. Randolph," Nyx said, "I accidentally ran into him and dropped my books. I had Psybolt's character sheet in those books. Randolph picked it up. In fact, he even read the name to me and commented on it."

"So Anthony Randolph does know about Psybolt," said Max, "and his number one flunky shows up here, watching us the day my shop burns down. Quite the coincidence, hm?"

When the police officer arrived, Max told him about Rex Riley's presence in the café, and how he was a wanted fugitive. Nyx pondered if the cop wondered why a comic book shop owner would know about wanted fugitives, but it didn't come up.

Now Rex and Randolph were together again removing all doubt that it could conceivably be a coincidence. They were working together, but for what goal? Nyx wished he was a fly on the wall in that counselor's office, but he did not want to push his luck. Max's warning rang in his ears, so, instead, he headed to the cafeteria.

Picking up his tray with the scoop of spaghetti on it, Nyx could hear his brothers arguing already.

"Why won't you go, Nigel?" Westley asked.

Nyx knew right away that the topic was the Munroe girls.

"I don't want to, Westley," said Nigel, firmly.

"Please. I'm begging," he said.

"Why do you want to go so badly?" Nigel asked.

"I just do," Westley answered, "Come on."

"No."

"Hey guys," Nyx said, hoping for a respite from the debate. Nyx did find it odd that Westley wanted to go to this dance as badly as he did. Westley liked Novella, but this was bordering on obsessive. Westley *could* be obsessive, but not about a girl.

"Hey, Nyx," said Nigel, happy for the distraction.

"Guess who I saw talking to Mr. Randolph a few minutes ago?" Nyx asked.

"Who?" Nigel replied, smiling a sneering smile at his twin.

"Rex Riley," Nyx said.

"No way!" blurted Nigel.

"Here?" Westley said, changing topics in his head.

"Yes," Nyx continued, "they're in the guidance office right now. And Rex looked pretty upset."

"What about Randolph?" Nigel said.

"He wasn't too excited to be seen with him," Nyx said. "He was acting like someone who had something to hide."

"Which he is," said Westley.

"Nyx, do you think he was the person who ransacked the living room?" Nigel inquired.

"Could be," Nyx said, but there were nagging questions bothering him.

"Should we call the police?" Nigel asked.

"Heads up… Uber Geek coming," Westley warned.

Julian walked with a purpose toward the Brothers Geek. Stopping beside their table, Julian averted his eyes preventing any eye contact with any of the Grimm brothers. Julian stood beside the table for a moment, saying nothing.

"Awkward silence!" Nigel blurted, breaking the dead air. Nyx once again frowned at his brother, but Nigel never seemed to catch on.

"Nyx," Julian finally said, "Mr. Randolph said he spoke to you."

"He did," Nyx said.

Tension choked the table, as Julian swayed from foot to foot.

"Um… Mr. Randolph thinks I should apologize," said Julian. "So… sorry."

"Boy, that's sincere," a sarcastic Nigel said.

Westley elbowed his twin in the ribs.

"And I'm sorry, Westley," said Julian, turning from Nyx. "I shouldn't have involved you in our problem. I'm truly sorry if you were terrorized."

Westley didn't say anything. Julian's candor to Westley was more genuine than his words to Nyx. Westley truly was an innocent victim in all this.

"Anyway," Julian said, "maybe I'll see you guys around."

"Sure," Nyx said coldly as Julian left the cafeteria.

"Do you believe that guy?" Nigel said. "He's got some nerve."

"He certainly still blames you, Nyx," said Westley, stating the obvious.

"Yeah… as apologies go… epic fail," Nigel said.

"It's not like we have to be friends," Nyx said. "With any luck, if nothing else, he won't be looking for revenge, and we can get back to normal."

"And what would that be like?" Nigel asked. "I think that our days of 'normal' are long passed."

Nyx couldn't disagree with Nigel. His point was valid. Nyx knew he was the Conduit, and, by definition, he would always be dealing with visions and mysterious messages. Normal would not involve such things.

"Understood," said Nyx, "but at least we could be as normal as possible. If nothing else, we could remove the tension here at school. Being able to stop worrying about watching over our shoulders for the Uber Geek… well, that would be well worth a truce."

Nigel and Westley stared past Nyx, mouths agape with scandal in their eyes. The twins were paralyzed with uncertainty.

"What's wrong?" Nyx said, noticing his brother's comatose visages. "Guys?"

Nyx did not want to look behind him. He had no idea what horror approached them that would cause his brothers to go into such an unresponsive state. The answer was more fearful than any Uber Geek sighting.

"I love your glasses," from behind him, said the distinctly feminine voice as slim fingers with blackened nails removed them from Nyx's face. "Let me try them on, cutie."

Nyx knew that the nagging question would not be answered by turning around, but that did not stop him. The blur that stood before him had an explicit dark tone to it.

"You have terrible vision, don't you? I can't see anything through these," the girl's voice said, as Nyx squinted, desperately trying to determine who had blinded him.

As the blur began to extend toward him, Nyx realized that she was going to put his glasses back on his face. Holding still and closing his eyes, Nyx felt the frame back in its proper place. Opening his eyes, the young geek was stunned by who he saw.

"Um… hi?" Nyx said

"Hi, Nyx," she said. The sensual shape of Helena Blood stood before him. A sly black-painted smile crossed her face, highlighting the hoop pierced through her bottom lip. "Can I join you?"

Her jet-black dyed hair glistened in the cafeteria light as it hung down her shoulders, slightly obscuring the spider tattoo that crawled from her long neck up to her lower left jaw.

Not sure how to respond, Nyx said, "Yeah."

Brushing against him, Helena squeezed onto the seat jutting from the oval lunchroom table. She bit her bottom lip playfully.

"I've been keeping an eye on you," she said.

"Huh?" Nyx replied, without even the slightest smoothness.

"Yes. Ever since you saved your brother and saved that football player… I find that so sexy. I love a hero."

Nyx gulped loudly. He was confused by her presence at the table. Helena Blood was a junior, and he never thought that she had ever even known that he existed. Her Goth appearance was strange, but there was no denying that she was hot.

"I was wondering," she said, pausing a moment. Nyx couldn't help but notice the pierced tongue as she spoke. "I was hoping… that you would come to the Sadie Hawkins dance with me."

Stunned, Nyx tried to speak, but the words did not form. He felt silly sitting in the cafeteria with this beautiful girl asking him on a date and being unable to respond.

"Um… ok," Nyx finally said, barely getting the few syllables out.

"Cool," she said, a smile brightening her face. She stood from the table, leaned down and kissed Nyx on the cheek. The feel of the cold metal from her ring pressed against his face. A smudge of black lipstick remained as proof of the event. With a wink, Helena was gone as quickly as she had arrived.

Nyx held his cheek in shock. He blinked a couple of time, trying to focus. He wanted to make sure that what had just happened actually *did* happen.

"What was that?" Nigel said.

"Yeah," said Westley, "She knows you?"

"Did you just agree to go to the dance with Helena Blood?" asked Nigel.

"I think so," Nyx said, still with a glassy look. Skepticism suddenly seized him. "She asked me, didn't she?"

"That's what it sounded like," said Westley.

"And I said yes?" said Nyx, piecing it together.

"Kind of," said Nigel.

"So I haven't lost my mind?" Nyx asked.

"Unless we all have," Nigel said.

Nyx tried to ponder the meaning for a minute, but it all was so surreal. Nyx had had no intention of going to this dance. He did not expect anyone to ask him. He had planned on staying home on Saturday and attempt to improve his level on Black Ops. Now, without warning, he had a social calendar. He wasn't sure what to do.

"Now that Nyx is going to the dance," said Westley, "you can agree to go and all three of us can attend."

"Forget it, Westley," said Nigel

"Why not?" begged Westley.

"I don't want to go," Nigel said.

Here they go again, thought Nyx.

Standing up to dump the remainder of the spaghetti on his tray, Nyx replayed the moment in his mind, and it always ended the same unexpected way…with him having a date with Helena Blood for the Sadie Hawkins dance.

"Hey, Nyx!"

Nyx looked in the direction where his name was called. Noah Ridge, with his arm draped over his girlfriend Penny Harris, was waving at him. Nyx smiled and moved over to the quarterback.

"Hey, Nyx, how's it going?" Noah asked.

"Helena Blood just asked me to the dance," he said, still in shock.

"Well alright, stud!" Noah said smacking Nyx on the back. The blow jarred him and snapped him out of his self-imposed trance. "Helena Blood is hot!"

Penny's head snapped quickly toward Noah, and she glared at him. Noah understood immediately that he was in trouble.

"But she is nothing compared to you, sweetie," Noah said, kissing Penny softly.

"Nyx," Penny said, after shaking her head at Noah's attempt to smooth things over, "I didn't know you were seeing anyone."

"I wasn't… I'm not," Nyx said. "She just came over to me and asked me out."

"That's strange. She is an odd girl, but I must confess that I don't know much about her. Why did she want to go to the dance with you?"

"Babe, don't rain on his parade," Noah said. "Good for you, Nyx."

"I didn't mean to suggest that…" Penny said, stopping. "I guess I'm just being paranoid. She couldn't have asked a kinder, sweeter person."

"Yeah, and if you need any pointers," Noah said just prior to taking a smack from Penny across his chest. "Ow. Stop it."

"I'm surprised about it, too," said Nyx. "It doesn't seem real."

"We'll be at the dance, Nyx," said Noah, "so if you need us, we'll be there for you."

Noah waited for the next expectant blow from Penny, but it did not come. Penny was nodding her head in agreement.

"Thanks. I have to get to class. See you guys later," said Nyx, moving down the hall. Penny and Noah kissed again, and they separated to head to their own classes.

Helena Blood stepped out from around the corner, and she smiled at the conversation. She ducked inside the janitor's closet.

"Well?" said Julian, who waited for her inside. "Did he accept?"

"Do you even need to ask?" Helena said.

She slinked over to him and followed that with an embrace. The two of them kissed passionately. Curiosity pulled them apart.

"Will you explain to me now why you wanted me to ask Nyx Grimm to the dance?" Helena asked. Helena's deep blue eyes searched Julian's features for the answer to the question that nagged at her, finding only an emotionless poker face. "It better be worth my while."

"It will be," Julian said. "You just have to be patient. It's a slow burn."

Chapter Nine

Emotional Rescue

"You can't handle the truth!"

-Col. Nathan Jessup

A Few Good Men

Grimm Household

Basement

Wednesday, 4:30 PM

The reflection told a depressing story, and despite flexing the twig-like arms and attempting a half-hearted most-muscular pose, the story's main idea would not change.

"Why did she ask me?" the shirtless Nyx asked himself, wishing he could find a suitable answer in his bathroom mirror, but knowing that his quest would end unfulfilled.

Taking out his tooth brush, Nyx polished his perfectly straight teeth as he did several times a day. The unfurling of the floss followed in his normal obsessive routine. Running his fingers across his dark, bristle covered scalp, Nyx flashed his best used car salesman smile at his mirror counterpart, trying to refrain from cracking up.

"Cutie?" he said, repeating the phrase used by Helena. Nyx didn't see it.

Pulling on his Weird Al concert shirt, Nyx was startled by the panicky shriek from upstairs.

"Nyx!Are you down there? Come up here!" yelled his mom. "Nyx!"

"Yeah!" Nyx responded. "Be there in a minute!"

Billie was not here when Nyx got home from school which had surprised him. She had been so smothering since the break-in that Nyx had considered her not being here a positive sign.

"Hurry up!" she screamed. Now… he wasn't so sure.

Nyx eased up the stairs with bewildered consternation. He was confused at the alarm being displayed in his mother's voice. *He hadn't done anything wrong*, he thought.

Billie stood at the top of the stairs with her arms crossed, and a scowl forming with each step she took. *Had he done something wrong?* Nyx thought.

"What's up, Mom?" Nyx said, without a care. He was trying to downplay whatever was causing her to be this angry. Plus, he really had no clue about what was going on.

"Nyx Grimm, where have you been?" she said, barely able to contain her acrimony. "I was going to pick you up tonight after school."

"What?" Nyx said, befuddled.

"Tonight! We talked about this!" she stated firmly.

"When?" Nyx asked, hoping to clear up the misunderstanding.

"This morning before you left," she said.

Nyx did not remember the conversation to which Billie was referring, but he had been pretty focused on the fire and Rex this morning. The prospect that he had missed her statement was strong.

"Sorry, Mom," Nyx said, "I must have spaced it off."

"Sorry's not good enough, Mister!" she said, her tense voice raising pitch. "I didn't know where you were, and with all the insanity lately… I was out of my mind with worry!"

What if she knew the whole story? Nyx thought.

Billie's eyes began to water up as she held both hands against her expanded stomach. Nyx felt guilty. He hated seeing his mother so upset.

"Sorry, Mom," Nyx said, softly, trying to emphasize his empathy. "I won't let it happen again."

Brushing away her salty secretion, Billie's sad eyes broke Nyx's heart. He wanted to say more, to make everything right, but he just did not understand why this was such a big deal. He had been getting himself home for quite a while now. Billie nodded at him, and she moved off to her room. Nyx leaned against the hand rail of the steps and watched as she closed the door.

"I know you're confused, Nyx," said his father as he walked into the room. Richard had just arrived home, and he had caught the end of the demonstration. "There is more going on here than just a break in."

Nyx's muscles went taut at his father's declaration, because he was worried what his dad meant. *MORE GOING ON* could apply to any number of details in Nyx's life. He tried replaying the words in his head to search for which words his dad had emphasized or for any hidden meanings. Failing that, Nyx decided on a direct approach.

"What do you mean?" he asked.

Richard glanced at their bedroom door as thoughts and memories raced back to the police officer. Removing his "utility" belt and taking his gun to the safe, Richard looked back to his increasingly distressed son.

"Go down to your room. I'll be down in a minute," Richard said.

This did not make Nyx feel better. The sensation of being condemned like a death row inmate could not be shaken as Nyx retreated to the safety of his basement room. Richard had been investigating the fire at Bright's Comix. *Could he have discovered a connection to me?* Nyx thought. *Had he discovered the secret that Nyx had been venturing to keep hidden?*

With an unlimited conglomeration of scenarios venturing through his over-active imagination, Nyx built his stress level to epic proportions posthaste. Trying to remain calm, Nyx laid on his bed, gazing into the ceiling tiles that have seen him to sleep since their move to Parker's Point.

A soft tap from Richard signaled his arrival. Walking into his son's room, Richard sat beside his computer desk in Nyx's leather desk chair, angling it just properly to face Nyx. Richard's attention was drawn to Nyx's mini-bust statue of Thor that sat on the desk. Picking it up, Richard examined the features and the long blonde hair of the Scandinavian thunder god.

"This is well done," he said, off topic. "Thor was always my favorite Avenger."

"Dad," Nyx said. Nyx understood that his own geekness was in all likelihood a genetic trait, but the flutter in his chest told him that this was not the moment to discuss Bowen Designs.

"Sorry," his dad said. "Your room is full of so many wonderful distractions. I didn't mean to digress. I need to talk to you."

"Yes," a nervous Nyx replied.

"I think you've noticed that your mother has been acting a little overprotective since the break in," he started.

"Huh?" Nyx said. He was not expecting that.

"I want you to understand why," he said.

Exhaling in relief that this wasn't about him, Nyx rolled over onto his stomach, supporting his head on his wrists. The clasp of dread had passed, replaced with the poke of intrigue. Nyx had noticed his mother's odd behavior, and now, perhaps, he would get some answers.

"When your mother was a child," Richard began, "around ten years old… she was accidentally left at her home alone… not a small feat considering she has four other sisters. Anyway, she was there alone when someone broke into the house."

Nyx was horrified at the idea. It was just like Westley.

"The guy was some thug who was looking for some quick cash. At least that is what they believe, since he hadn't taken any of the others valuables in their house. Billie was in the room that she shared with your Aunt Nicole, and she could hear him tearing things apart. She could not reach the phone, and she was too scared to try to climb from her second floor window, so she hid in her closet."

Richard retrieved the Thor bust and began fiddling with it again. He was still conflicted about revealing this secret, and he hoped that in doing so, he wasn't damaging his marriage further.

"She was scared," he said, continuing. "The noises came closer with each passing second. Crashes and bangs… and Billie was in her closet, in the dark, alone and afraid."

Nyx sat up on the bed. He was enthralled with the story, but he was troubled about what his father was going to say next.

"Then the guy came into her room," he said.

Oh no, Nyx thought.

"Your mom peeked out through the slits in the closet door. She doesn't remember what he looked like… just that he was big," Richard said. "She blocked that out."

"Who was he?" Nyx inquired.

"We don't know. He was never caught," answered Richard. "I think that has been part of the problem."

"Then what happened," Nyx asked intently, though he did not really want to know.

"He was going through her room as she watched him… she couldn't breathe. She watched him as he moved closer to the closet. As his frame blocked the light from the room, his large, hairy hand reached for the closet door. Just as he was about to grasp the door handle, there was a scream from downstairs. Her older sister Clarissa had found the mess downstairs and was calling the police. The man quickly escaped out their bedroom window."

"Wow," Nyx said.

"Billie was terribly traumatized by that day. To her credit, she didn't let it completely rule her life, but I do think that, when we first met, the fact that I had just been accepted to the police academy was a big selling point," Richard said with a small chuckle.

"So the other day was the second time…" Nyx started.

"Third."

Richard spun around in the computer chair to see his wife standing unexpectedly by the doorway. Nyx was so engrossed by his father's tale that he had not seen or heard Billie enter the room, and he was unsure how much of their conversation she had caught.

"We had been married just about six months," she said, slowly walking beside Richard. Billie held her hand out to her husband, and he eagerly took it. Calmness surrounded her that Nyx hadn't seen for several days. It was a welcome change.

"I'm sorry, honey," said Richard.

"I know. So am I," she responded.

"I thought he should know," he said.

"You're right," she said.

"You're not mad?" Richard said.

"Mad? No. Maybe hormonal."

Richard snickered at her self-deprecating remark. She bent down and kissed him tenderly.

"Ugh… I'm still in the room," Nyx said, making a face. Although he responded like a typical teenager, Nyx was ecstatic that their fighting was at an end.

Ending the kiss, Billie gave her attention to Nyx.

"Six wonderful months of marital bliss, and then it happened again," she said.

"This time we returned from the movies," Richard continued, "to find our apartment had been burglarized."

"Did you catch that guy?" Nyx asked with a glimmer of optimism.

"No, I'm afraid not," Richard said. "It was Chicago, and the police… we did all we could, but the sad fact is… sometimes the police can only do so much."

"That… violation," said Billie, after searching for the right word, "took me right back to that closet. The fear… the loneliness. It was as if that day had just happened."

"Then it happened for a third time here," said Richard.

"And this time it was way worse than either of the others," Billie said.

"Why?" Nyx inquired.

"Because this wasn't just about me, and what had happened to me as a child. This was about my own children. Westley was here alone, and anything could have happened to him. Any of you could have been here. If anything would have happened to any of my children, I don't know how I could go on."

Richard affectionately kissed Billie's hand in support as his wife recounted her painful worries in an attempt to help their eldest son fathom that her recent behavior wasn't as erratic as it once seemed.

"It didn't help that this break-in had some connection to you, Nyx," said Billie. "That *Psybolt* reference was so specific that it only served to amplify my already raging paranoia, especially after that whole horrible incident with Julian."

"And I didn't help either," said Richard. "I was far from sympathetic. I had hoped that I would never have to see your mother that afraid again, and I did not react well. I'm so sorry, Billie."

Nyx digested everything his parents had told him, and he tried to assimilate the knowledge into the current situation. Nyx wasn't sure how it all fit together.

"Are you alright?" Billie asked her son.

"Yes," he said, a thought popping into his head. "Actually, I had a surprise invitation today. I was asked to the dance on Saturday."

Nyx's risky announcement felt out of place, and he wished that he had not said anything as soon as the words had come out of his mouth.

"Really?" Billie said.

"Yes," said Nyx, deciding that since the cat was out of the bag, he may as well press on. "Her name is Helena, and she asked me at lunch."

"Under the circumstances," Richard said, trying to gauge the reaction of his wife, "that might not be the best idea, son."

"But Dad…"

"We need to take your mother's concerns seriously. She is right… whomever broke in here did appear to be targeting you."

"Now Richard," Billie said, changing her tune, "I don't want Nyx to miss out on his first dance here because of my irrational fears."

"The fears are not irrational, Billie. Someone did break in here," he said.

"Yes," she said, thinking a bit. She was concerned.

"I didn't think you liked dances, Nyx," questioned Richard.

Nyx had, in fact, attended several Middle School dances before they moved to Parker's Point, although never with a date. He had never had a good time. The dances were always full of melodrama that only teenagers could provide.

"And who is this Helena?" Richard asked.

"She's a girl at school," Nyx said, deciding that the gothic image would be a detail to save for a later time.

"And you want to go?" a hopeful Billie asked.

"I said I would," Nyx said, though that was not an actual answer to the question.

"Then that's settled," Billie said. "I would never forgive myself if my baggage prevented my son from going to something fun and enjoyable."

"Are you sure, Billie?" Richard asked. "I have to work. Will you be alright home with Nyx out?"

Contemplation blanketed Billie like the winter's first snowfall, and her final culmination was as bright as the white, frozen precip.

"I received an e-mail from Nyx's school yesterday requesting that I act as a chaperone for the dance. I had planned on turning them down, but, if I agree, I can be there to keep an eye on him," Billie said.

An insincere smile became Nyx's façade as his most fervent desire had suddenly metamorphosed into being a good enough actor to keep his parents from seeing his true feelings on that idea. If this helped his mom, then Nyx was for it despite the potential embarrassment alert rating being red… bright red.

"This is good news, Nyx. I'm feeling better already," she said.

"The twins are thinking about going as well," Nyx said, throwing his brothers to the wolves.

"All three of my boys? Goodness gracious…" Billie said, turning to leave the room. She stopped for a moment and turned back to Nyx. "Thank you for understanding, Nyx, and for putting up with me."

Billie headed out of the room. The anxiety of the last few days was suppressed by the thought of her three sons going through one of life's momentous occasions. Richard watched her leave and smiled.

"Thank you, Nyx. You're my boy," he said, very proud of his son.

"Thanks, Dad," Nyx said, as his father stood up and started to leave.

"Oh," Richard said, halting his progress, "I was wondering if you could help me out. I would really like to catch the person who ransacked the house… to give your mom some closure finally, but I am at a loss. I know this *Psybolt* was a character that you made for your role-playing game. Could I see your character sheet?"

"Sure," Nyx said. He reached under the bed and grabbed his brown accordion file where he kept all of his gaming materials. Characters from *Dungeons and Dragons*, *Champions*, and *Vampire: The Masquerade* were stored in this file in case Nyx needed one for a game.

Nyx found something odd about the accordion file. It was lighter than it should be. Unlashing the string that kept it shut, Nyx opened the file with urgency and reached inside.

"Is something wrong?" Richard asked, observing the strange reaction that his son had to grabbing the file.

Nyx pulled out the only character sheet that remained inside the brown storage unit. It was Psybolt. None of the other 30 or so characters that Nyx had created and written up on their own character sheets were in the file. There was only Psybolt.

"Nyx?" Richard said further wondering about the mysterious turmoil that had enchanted Nyx. "Are you okay?"

"Yeah, I'm fine," he said, regaining his sensibility. "Here he is."

Nyx handed his dad Psybolt's character sheet. Nyx didn't need it anymore. For one, he would never play this character again, and secondly, even if he did, he knew Psybolt's characteristics and backstory by heart. There was no reason to continue to keep the sheet.

"Thanks," Richard said, taking the sheet. He studied Nyx carefully. "Are you sure you are alright?"

"I'm fine, Dad. There's nothing to worry about. I was just thinking about Mom," lied Nyx.

Taking Nyx's lie at face value, Richard took the sheet and left the room. Nyx immediately looked back inside the accordion file, as if he could have missed the papers the first time. It was completely empty now, and Nyx had not touched this file since before the incident with Julian. Several possible answers swirled around Nyx's mind, but one kept coming back to the forefront. And it was a disturbing one.

The shredded paper that was left on the floor of the living room after it was ransacked. Could it be the other characters from the file? If that were true, Nyx could only think of one thing....

The person who broke into the house had been in his room.

Chapter Ten

An Upsetting Discovery

"Snakes... why'd it have to be snakes."

-Indiana Jones

Raiders of the Lost Ark

Grimm Household

Nyx's bedroom

Thursday morning, 7:05 AM

"Now, I just want everyone to be absolutely clear and understand what I am asking you. It is important. Did any of you touch this file recently?" interrogated Nyx.

Westley and Nigel sat on Nyx's bed on either side of Ariel. All three were concentrating on the brown accordion file their brother held.

"I keep it under my bead," Nyx continued. "Did anyone here touch it?"

"Why would we want to touch your stupid brown thingy?" Ariel said. "It's boring and stupid."

"So Ariel didn't touch it. What about you guys?" Nyx persisted.

"Why would we?" Nigel said, incredulously. "Don't you keep your RPG characters in that? We don't role-play... I mean... not with paper and pencil. Computer, on-line, now that's different! Now you're getting somewhere... but PnP? How ...yesterday."

"I know... I just needed to be sure," Nyx said.

"Can I go now?" an impatient Ariel blurted.

"Yes," Nyx answered.

"Finally!" she bellowed, full of dramatics. It was as if the five minutes in Nyx's room had been a life sentence for the young girl. She ran from the room before her brother changed his mind.

"What's this really about?" asked Westley as soon as his sister was out of earshot,

"All my characters are gone... except for Psybolt. Someone is trying to send me a message," Nyx said.

"What do you think happened to them?" asked Nigel.

"Do you remember the shredded paper on the floor of the living room after it had been vandalized?"

"No way!" exclaimed Nigel.

"Are you sure?" Westley said in a pessimistic tone.

"Sure? Of course I'm not sure. There's no way to be sure. But I can't come up with a more reasonable answer, can you?" Nyx said.

"What about Mom?" Westley offered, but they all knew that their mother had a lot of respect for their property. So much so that she even generally allowed things to pile up before she would step in. There was no way she would have cleaned out a file that was as a carefully organized as this one had been.

"Not Mom. Dad was here when I took it out, and he said nothing. If it wasn't you guys or me, I only have one other choice," Nyx reasoned.

"So what are you going to do?" asked Westley, looking timid.

"I don't know. The Psybolt character sheet was left behind for a reason. So that must hold the key. I hope to see Max today or tomorrow and maybe he'll have some ideas."

"Shouldn't you guys be getting to school to work on the school's computers?" reminded Westley of the "punishment" served.

"Yeah," Nyx replied, returning the file beneath the bed. "Mom's giving us a ride this morning."

"By the way, Nyx," said Nigel, "thanks for siccing Mom on me last night. She came into our room all spazzed out about the dance."

"Better you than me," laughed Nyx.

"But I'm not going, and you are," Nigel said.

"Come on, Nigel," Westley whined. "Please."

"No," he replied.

"Please."

"No."

"Please."

"No."

"Let's go, guys," Nyx said, herding the twins out of his bedroom.

Parker's Point High School

Mrs. Templeton's Science Class

Thursday, 8:20 AM

"Good morning, Nyx," Mandy said, sitting in her chair beside him at the black topped science table.

"Morning, Mandy," responded Nyx.

An anxious energy exuded from the teenager as she slid her chair into the table. The mix of anticipation and fear was new for her as she ran the words through her head. She had been practicing this conversation for the last couple of days, but she had not found that perfect combination of syllables. She told herself that she would procrastinate no more. Today would be the day.

"Carpe diem," she said, beneath her breath.

"What?" asked Nyx, not sure if she had said something.

"Nothing," she said, pushing ahead. "So… what did you think about that Sadie Hawkins dance?"

Clumsy, she thought. Mandy had hoped to be so much smoother than that. However, the moment had passed and there was no stopping now.

"Yeah," said Nyx, "I'm going."

Those words struck Mandy like a boxer's hook to the midsection as she felt the wind rush from her.

"What?" she gasped.

"Helena Blood asked me yesterday at lunch," Nyx said, and, jokingly, he added, "and don't sound so shocked."

"No… I didn't mean," Mandy said, retreating verbally. She never expected that someone would beat her to it. She didn't know she was in a race.

"That's okay," Nyx said with a wink. "I was shocked too."

"Helena Blood?" Mandy repeated, just to make sure this wasn't some kind of delusion that she was having.

"I know what you're thinking," Nyx said.

"You do?" Mandy asked, flummoxed.

"You're thinking... why would Helena Blood want to go to the dance with Nyx?" he said.

"No, I'm not," she said.

"You're not? Well, I am," he laughed.

"Quite the opposite, I'm wondering why you would want to go to the dance with her," Mandy retorted.

"Why **wouldn't** I?" Nyx said, not knowing that his response was a poor one.

"She's kind of... weird, isn't she?" Mandy said.

"Why would I, of all people, hold that against her? Plus, she's hot," Nyx said to the disappointment of Mandy. She had believed that Nyx was above such a thing. "I mean, yeah, the piercings and the tattoo... they're uncommon, but I learned a lesson about judging people by their appearance or by my preconceived notions."

"Oh," Mandy replied, a little ashamed of herself.

"Plus... she's hot," Nyx repeated with a lilt. Nyx then asked, obliviously, "Are you going to ask someone to go with you?"

"I was thinking about it," Mandy said sadly, as Mrs. Templeton began the daily lesson.

Nyx couldn't believe his eyes.

Nigel was walking arm in arm with Jenette Munroe.

No way! Nyx thought.

"Nigel!" Nyx yelled to get his brother's attention as he hurried after the couple. "Hey!"

Nyx wanted to be sensitive, but the constant refusals that had crossed his brother's lips over the last few days rang in his head. Nyx had to know what was going on.

"What's new, Nigel?" Nyx said, trying to be subtle, but failing miserably. "Hi, Jenette."

"Nothing," Nigel said, as if nothing out of the ordinary had occurred. Nyx had to take a moment to make sure that his jaw was closed.

"Nothing?" said Nyx, tilting his head slightly toward Jenette. "Really?"

"Oh, you mean Jenette," Nigel said, brashly. Nyx turned an embarrassing shade of red. "She asked me to go to the dance, and I accepted."

"I thought you didn't want to go to the dance," Nyx said, trying to be as diplomatic as he could.

"That was when Westley was asking me," he said.

"Does Westley know?" Nigel asked.

"Not yet. I plan on torturing him some first, so nothing out of you, understand?" Nigel sneered.

"So," Nyx said, processing, "Jenette asked you this morning?"

"Yes, Nyx," Jenette continued, a little irritated at the conversation not including her. "I saw Nigel in Mr. Randolph's office this morning, and I asked him to go, and he said yes."

"I wanted **her** to ask me, not as a favor to Westley," Nigel said, explaining.

"Wait," Nyx said, distracted. "You were in Mr. Randolph's office this morning?"

`"Yes," Nigel said. "He had some more computer questions for me."

"And… that's where you asked him?" Nyx questioned.

"Yes, I said that already. Try to keep up, okay?" she snarled.

Before Nyx's suspicions could flare up more, a soft arm with an elbow length black glove wrapped around Nyx's upper chest and neck, and the fragrance of honey filled the air.

"Hey, cutie," Helena said, whispering in his ear. "Whatcha doing?"

"Oh," Nyx said, startled by Helena's arrival and public display of affection. He blushed again, redder than before, at the "cutie" comment. "Hi, Helena. Nothing. Just talking to my brother."

"Hello," she said to Nigel, "I'm sorry, which one are you?"

"Nigel," he said.

"Of course…Nigel. Hello," she said with a touch of condemnation. Helena turned her attention back to Nyx. "Will you walk with me?"

"Sure," Nyx replied. "See you later, Nigel. Jenette."

Taking his hand, Helena led Nyx off, strolling through the hallway. The two of them brought a fair share of whispering, giggling and pointing. Helena dispatched each one with an evil eye or a raised eyebrow. Nyx was impressed with how she handled herself among the gossipmongers and the judgment peddlers of the high school scene. Her attitude screamed *talk about me at your own risk.* It was a confidence that Nyx had always lacked, especially in any social setting. He never moved carefree down the halls at school. There were just too many pratfalls. He found it rather appealing.

"Say," said Helena, pointing up ahead. "There's the auditorium. That's where you saved your other brother, right?"

"Well… that's one way of looking at it," Nyx fumbled, remembering that, much like the Cavalry, it was actually Coach Cook and his football team that saved the day.

"Show me around," she said, pulling him toward the auditorium door.

"We should really get to class," Nyx said, checking his cell phone for the time.

"Poppycock," she said, "they won't miss us. You can tell me about your adventure first hand."

Reluctantly, Nyx followed behind Helena although he wasn't sure he had much of a choice as the grip on his hand was clamped like the tightest vise.

To Nyx's chagrin, the auditorium door was unlocked. Walking slowly down the darkened aisle brought the memories of that day flooding back to the young geek. The recollection of Westley bound and gagged and hanging above the stage as Julian made threats still sent chills across him.

"So what was it like?" Helena asked as the red tint of the security lights amidst the darkness illuminated her pallid features.

"It was like it wasn't real. It felt more like a movie," Nyx said, as they continued walking down the aisle. "Julian was my best friend, and he was acting like someone I didn't know. It was like he wasn't himself. But he was."

"Really?" she said, absorbed by his words.

"He did everything because he was obsessed with Penny Harris," Nyx said.

"Penny?"

"Yes, I couldn't believe what he tried to do. He physically threatened Westley if I didn't help clear his name. Westley who had never done anything to him... heck, Westley and Nigel idolized Julian. They called him the Uber Geek."

Helena chuckled at the name, but she was listening to every single word of Nyx's intense story.

"Do you have a brother or a sister?" asked Nyx.

"No," she answered, "I'm an only child."

"That's too bad. Don't tell my brothers this, because I'll just deny it, but I don't know what I would do without them."

"That's sweet," Helena said, "I sometimes wish I had a sibling."

"Don't get me wrong, they can be a huge pain in the butt... a lot of the time," Nyx said. "Okay... most of the time, but they're my brothers. I just couldn't imagine my life without them, and I couldn't believe Julian would go out of his way to target them."

"That doesn't sound..." Helena stopped in midsentence and let out a blood curdling scream that echoed through the empty auditorium.

"Helena?" Nyx said, confused by her sudden scream.

She turned to Nyx and practically leaped into his arms. She screamed again, her body quivering badly. The sudden onset of the fit of terror threw Nyx off his guard.

"What is it, Helena? What..."

Nyx didn't need to finish his question as he witnessed what had set Helena off. In the third row of seats on her side of the aisle there was a slumped body wedged into a seat. A dark stream of plasma had dripped from the man and pooled up on the floor beside it. The darkness obscured

91

any other details from the pair. Nyx started to pull away from her clench only to receive opposition.

"No no no," cried Helena, grasping tighter.

"Helena," Nyx said, breaking free and grasping her by both shoulders. He looked deeply into her troubled eyes. "I need you to go get Mrs. Kendrick or Mr. Stanton."

The firm, in-control tone was in stark contrast with Nyx's insecurities in the hallway, and Helena was grateful Nyx was here and able to take charge. She wouldn't have believed this was the same, intimidated boy who blabbered through her invitation to the dance yesterday. As she started up the aisle, Nyx moved into the row.

"You aren't going to touch him?" she said with a gruesome shudder.

"He could still be alive, and I could help," he said. "Go… get help now."

As Helena ran out of the auditorium, Nyx inched closer to the man. Using the light from his cell phone, Nyx realized two things. One, seeing the gaping wound to the man's head, he was beyond help, and, two, this was Rex Riley.

"Oh my God," Nyx said, the terrorist's fate bringing new level of uneasiness to what was going on.

Scanning around the body, the gun gripped tightly in Rex's right hand immediately drew Nyx's attention. Rex was slumped to the left with his right arm draped over the seat beside him. A piece of paper that stuck noticeably out of Rex's shirt pocket beaconed to Nyx. He snatched the paper, unfolded it quickly, and read the handwritten note.

To the world,

I have done too many terrible things. I cannot face the guilt over the horrors any longer. Wrecking the Grimm's living room and torching Bright's Comix will be the last of my evil deeds. I hope the next life will be better. I'm sorry for the pain I have caused.

R. Riley

"I can't believe this," Nyx said, re-reading the note. Nyx searched through the context trying to make this make sense. Nyx found it difficult to believe that the person Max had described to him, suddenly found a conscience because of an act of vandalism and an act of arson.

"Mr. Grimm! What are you doing?" said Principal Kendrick as the main lights of the auditorium turned on. Helena followed behind her slowly as the principal hurried with purpose down the aisle. Helena sat in one of the rear rows, hanging her head. She looked as if she was crying. "Don't touch anything! You should know better than that!"

"It's a suicide note," Nyx said, holding the paper out toward Mrs. Kendrick. She held her hands up in front of her.

"Put it back where you found it. The police won't want you contaminating the scene," she said. "They may want to check for fingerprints."

"Too late for that," Nyx said, noticing that he had stepped in blood. "I had to see if I could help him."

Mr. Stanton, who had entered from a different way in order to turn the auditorium lights on, walked out onto the stage.

"What's the status, Mrs. Kendrick?" Mr. Stanton, the vice-principal, asked.

"It looks like a suicide, though I don't know who he is," she said, trying to get a good look at Rex's face.

"His name is Rex Riley," Nyx said. "He's a friend of Mr. Randolph."

Nyx decided not to go into any more details about his knowledge of Rex Riley. He figured that the details would become known now sooner than later.

"How do you know that?" Mr. Stanton asked.

"I saw him... talking to Mr. Randolph yesterday near his office," Nyx said, again omitting the fact that they appeared to be arguing.

"Mr. Stanton, why don't you go get Mr. Randolph," Mrs. Kendrick said as Nyx fought the urge to smile. "The police should be here momentarily."

"Right," Mr. Stanton said. "Nyx, why don't you go have a seat with Ms. Blood. I'm sure the police will have some questions for you when they get here."

Nyx walked back up the aisle, sitting in the seat beside Helena. Tremors surged through her limbs as she was unable to control them. Awkwardly, Nyx placed his arm around her shoulders. Helena settled her head against his chest.

"I- I've never seen a dead body before," she admitted.

"Me either," said Nyx.

"You're kidding," she said, lifting her head from its resting place. "You sure fooled me. I got the impression that this was all second nature to you."

Helena returned her head to Nyx's chest. Her soft sobs caused dark streaks across her fair skin. Nyx couldn't explain it. It had to do with being the Conduit, and it helped knowing that the monster known as Rex Riley wouldn't hurt anyone again. Maybe those children in Scotland finally had some justice.

But it still didn't make sense. Rex Riley was a sociopath. He didn't feel guilt. That suicide note was just too bizarre and out of character for him.

"Wait," Nyx said, sitting up straight.

"What?" Helena asked.

"Fingerprints," Nyx repeated. Reaching into his pocket, Nyx pulled out his iPod. He began wiping it clean with his shirtsleeve.

"What are you doing?" Helena asked.

"Would you do something for me," Nyx asked, "without asking me a lot of questions?"

"I... guess," she said.

"I need you to distract Mrs. Kendrick," Nyx said, "just for a minute. Get her out of the auditorium."

"Why?"

"I need to get close to the body," he said.

Chapter Eleven

Scene of the Crime

"Murder, Murder
It's a right scare
Bloody murder
In the night!"

Murder, Murder
-A Newsboy and Ensemble
Jekyll & Hyde, the Broadway show

Frank Wildhorn & Leslie Bricusse

"Mrs. Kendrick," Helena said, still shaking and trying not to look at the body of Rex Riley, "can… can I talk to you privately for a minute?"

"Not now, Ms. Blood. I'm a little busy at this moment," the principal responded.

"Please?" Helena asked, the waterworks flowing freely from the young girl. She was quite convincing, and Nyx wasn't exactly sure how much of the display was acting. If it was an act, Helena Blood was a star.

"Now, now," Mrs. Kendrick said, embracing the troubled, yet overly dramatic teen. "I'm sorry. I know this was traumatic for you. Come here."

Mrs. Kendrick led Helena to the backstage area away from the prying eyes of anyone else. This was the opportunity Nyx Grimm had wanted when he enlisted the upset junior into his plot. Hurrying down to the body, Nyx reached and grabbed the terrorist's left hand, pressing its fingers onto his iPod. Carefully, Nyx took the electronic device and slipped it into his shirt pocket. His mission complete, Nyx quickly moved up the auditorium aisle when the rear doors opened.

Standing before Nyx was Mr. Randolph and Mr. Stanton. The counselor's red beard was more prominent against his severely pale face. This was something Nyx had not noticed before, but it seemed painfully apparent now. Wrinkles jutted away from his bloodshot eyes and the scars near his temples appeared larger than Nyx remembered. The pair's eyes met as Nyx's blood ran cold.

"Mr. Randolph, you look sick. Are you alright?" asked Nyx.

Ignoring his question, Randolph moved past the geek down toward the body of his childhood friend. Nyx thought whether Randolph was a better actor than Helena had been or if he was really upset with the fate of his comrade.

"Where were you going, Mr. Grimm?" Mr. Stanton inquired.

"I just wanted some air," said Nyx. "It's kind of creepy being here with a dead guy."

"Of course," he said, but Nyx got the impression that Mr. Stanton didn't believe him. "I'm sorry, but you need to stay here. The police are here now."

Nyx sat down again, now intently studying Anthony Randolph and his behavior. The counselor stood back away from the body, being sure not to touch anything. Then, he sat in the first chair directly opposite Rex. Feebly, he leaned his head back, staring at the lights. It was as if he did not even have the strength to hold his head upright.

Richard Grimm led several officers into the auditorium, except he veered off and found his son.

"Why do I have to keep being called to this school to find you in this auditorium?" Richard asked.

"I wish I knew," Nyx said.

"Are you alright, son?" Richard asked.

"Yes," said Nyx. That was true.

"What happened?" he asked.

"Helena and I found him," Nyx said.

"What were you doing in here?" he asked.

"Dad!" Nyx said, embarrassed by the question. Richard understood.

"So, you two came inside here..." Richard started.

"Helena wanted me to tell her about the thing with Julian," Nyx started, "and we came in here. As we were walking, Helena saw him and screamed."

"Where is Helena? I will need to talk to her too," Richard said.

"She's with Mrs. Kendrick. She's pretty shaken up."

"I'm not surprised," Richard said. "Then what?"

"I sent Helena to get help, and I checked the body."

"Nyx!" Richard said. "Why did you do that?"

"I wanted to help him, if I could," Nyx said. Richard sighed. He knew that his son had a good heart, and he wouldn't have expected anything less of him. "He was dead. Shot in the head. There was a note in his pocket..."

"Nyx, you didn't," said Richard.

"I did. It said he was the person who vandalized our house and torched Max's."

"What?" Richard's astonishment outweighed his feeling of being letdown by his son's mistake.

"I'm sorry Dad, but I couldn't help myself. I was curious."

"You shouldn't have done that, Nyx. Is there anything else?"

"It was dark in here, and I stepped in some blood as well," said Nyx.

"Of course you did," Richard said. "Mr. Stanton said you identified the man as Rex Riley. How did you know him?"

"I saw the name in the note," said Nyx, "and I recognized him from yesterday. I saw him talking to Mr. Randolph by his office."

"Aye, indeed the lad did, Officer Grimm," said Randolph, who had walked to the rear of the auditorium. "Rex Riley be a … were a childhood bloke o' me back in Scotland. The two o' us were close."

Randolph coldly glared toward Nyx. Randolph was displaying several of the classic symptoms of grief and sadness, but there was just something about him that made Nyx doubt his sincerity.

"What did Mr. Riley want to talk to you about yesterday, Mr. Randolph?" asked Richard.

"He be wanting me t' aid him. I don't know if you be knowin' this, but Rex be a dangerous man," Randolph said.

"Yes, I know that," Richard said. Nyx was surprised. "Rex Riley is an international terrorist. We had a report of him being in Parker's Point this week. So… what did he want with you?"

"He wanted me t'help him. He was out o' money, and he wanted to trade on me sweet memories. I told him that I would not be a helpin' him, and that I gave him twenty-four hours to turn himself in or I would be forced t'do it."

"Rex Riley, a 'dangerous man' as you said, came to the school, and you did not report it? You did not tell the principal or the police? How did you know that Riley wasn't going to do something tragic?"

"He told me that he be regretful for his crimes. He wanted to end the runnin' and be a better man, like the old days. I believed him. That be why I gave him the time frame. I wanted to give him time t'put his affairs in order. Had I known what he meant… I regret not sayin' anythin' now."

Nyx continued to observe Randolph during his dialogue with his father. Everything Randolph said was believable, but there was something in the inflection that made Nyx believe that there was more here than Randolph was saying. Add to the fact that Randolph did not resemble the same man that Nyx first met… bells were going off in Nyx's head.

"When was the last time you had seen Riley before yesterday?" asked Richard.

"Ah… it was years ago… in Glasgow, I believe. He was so different.

The boy I remembered was long gone. I had been thinkin' that I would never be seein' him again," said Randolph. "Then he showed up from nowhere, yesterday."

"Well, I'm sorry for your loss," said Richard.

Mrs. Kendrick came from the stage, with her arm around Helena. Spotting Richard talking with Mr. Randolph, she called out. The two of them walked over to the police officer as the other officers secured the body.

"Officer Grimm, this is Helena Blood. She was the first person to find the body along with Nyx," she said.

"Helena?" Richard said, looking at Nyx. His surprised look told Nyx that she wasn't what he expected. "Thank you for talking to me. I know this has been difficult."

"Officer Grimm?" Helena said, looking at Nyx.

"Yes, I am Nyx's father. I hope that does not make this more awkward," he said.

"No… it's okay. Nyx is really brave," she said.

"Yes, I know," Richard said. "How did the two of you wind up here?"

"It was my fault, Mr. Grimm. I wanted Nyx to show me where he saved his brother. I literally dragged him in here," she said. "He wanted to go to class. Then, I saw the …" Helena paused, closed her eyes, and tried to relax.

"Then what?" Richard asked.

"I screamed. Then Nyx took over. He calmed me down and sent me for help. Then he went to see if he could help the guy. I ran to the office and found Mrs. Kendrick and Mr. Stanton and told them what we found."

"Okay, why don't you and Nyx head back to class," said Richard.

Nyx got to his feet, and stepped into the aisle. The two kids walked out of the auditorium as a pair of police officers were starting to string yellow crime scene tape across the door.

"Are you okay?" Nyx said.

"I think so," she said. "I'm glad you were there."

"Thanks," Nyx said.

Parker's Point High School

Gymnasium

Thursday, 10:53 AM

Nyx sat in the crowd in the bleachers. Five minutes ago, an announcement came over the intercom system. Mrs. Kendrick had told the student body that there would be an assembly. She did not give specifics about what the assembly was about, but the rumors about the police cordoning off the auditorium had been swamping the school. Nyx had even heard some whispers about a dead body being found. He didn't tell anyone, and he couldn't believe that Helena was spreading it around, so he had no idea how the rumors had gotten out.

Nigel and Westley sat next to Nyx while he was searching the sea of faces for Helena. He did not find her.

"What's going on, Nyx. I saw Dad here," said Nigel.

"Why are you asking me?" Nyx said.

"Come on, aren't you always in the middle of everything?" Nigel said.

"Smart aleck," said Nyx.

"Am I lying?" he said.

"No," Nyx said, admitting the truth.

"So…"

"Helena and I found Rex Riley," Nyx whispered, "…dead."

"What?" Westley said. Westley had been quiet since coming into the gym.

"No way!" Nigel exclaimed.

"I'll tell you guys about it later," said Nyx, hoping to avoid prying ears inside the gym.

"Come on Nyx, don't hold out on us," Nigel said.

"Later," Nyx said, spying Helena walking into the gym. She sat down on the corner of the bleachers, head down.

After a few minutes, the entire school had filtered into the last minute assembly, and the police tape across the auditorium door had created quite

100

the buzz throughout the gym. Nyx heard several wild rumors about what was going on, some close, some way out there.

Finally, Principal Kendrick, Mr. Stanton, and Mr. Randolph entered the gym, followed by the Superintendent of Parker's Point Schools, Mr. Battle.

Superintendent Tomas Battle was the only African-American superintendent in the state, a fact that for whichhe was admired. A veteran, Battle had lost his left eye in service to the country as a young man and wore an eye patch proudly. His dedication to country made him a hero to all of Parker's Point.

However, Nyx would forever remember him from their first meeting, when his entire family connected with him at orientation. Battle's cleanly shaven head and meticulously manicured beard inspired a great debate between Nigel and Westley.

Westley thought Battle looked exactly like Ultimate Nick Fury, and Nigel said he looked like a pirate. The argument raged for weeks.

Now Superintendent Battle approached the microphone, and Nyx could hear the debate beginning anew.

"I am guessing that there are plenty of rumors flying around the building about what has happened this morning," said Mr. Battle, "and why the police have closed off the auditorium. I am here to put all of those rumors to rest. This morning, the body of a man was discovered in the auditorium. At this point, the police believe this man to have committed suicide, though the investigation is on-going."

"He's taking charge just like Nick Fury would," whispered Westley.

"Give him a minute, and he'll finish with an 'arrrrr'," said Nigel.

"Forget pirates… ninjas are way cooler," said Westley. "I bet Nick Fury would make an awesome ninja!"

"Quiet guys, I want to hear this," said Nyx. *Ninjas?* Nyx thought. *Where'd that come from?*

"The man was a visitor to the town. He is not a local resident, nor did he work at the school," said Battle. "It is unclear why, if he did commit suicide, he chose to end his life in our school. Perhaps the police will be able to determine the specifics of the poor man's life and death. Either way, I would ask now if we could have a moment of silence for the life lost in our building."

Mr. Battle lowered his head, and the entire student body followed suit. Nyx couldn't believe that he was having a moment of silence honoring Rex Riley, a man responsible for the death of untold numbers of Scottish children, among countless other sins. However, he did it anyway. Even Westley and Nigel stopped their bickering to show respect for a life lost.

"Thank you," said Mr. Battle. "So now, I have the responsibility to inform you that, because of the investigation of the police, we will be dismissing school for today and will be canceling school tomorrow as well."

The explosive cheer from the masses nearly blew the roof off the gymnasium. Mr. Battle looked extremely irritated.

"I would hope that the loss of a human life is not a matter for celebration for any of you," chastised Mr. Battle. The disappointed scowl brought the entire gym to silence. "This man's life has ended, and you should not be rejoicing in this tragedy because you get some time off school. You should keep perspective on the situation. You should take the time off as a gift, and be thankful that you are alive, well, and count the blessings that you have."

The shame in the gym did not eclipse the joy of the students, though they did a better job of not showing how excited they were.

"So, come Monday, the school will be open once again," said Mr. Battle.

Monday? Nyx thought. *What about the dance?*

And Nyx was not the only student with the dance on their mind. A rumble of whispers began in the crowd and spread quickly. Mr. Battle gave way to Mrs. Kendrick. Mr. Randolph stood beside her at the microphone.

"I can hear the questions already. Let me assure you, we have no intention of canceling the Sadie Hawkins dance," she said, as an audible collective 'whew' from the student body rippled across the gym. "However, the gymnasium and the school grounds will be off-limits for the dance, so we have had to make some adjustments to the plans for Saturday night."

The mumblings began to increase as the collected teenagers were intrigued by the words spoken by their illustrious leader.

"That is when Mr. Randolph stepped in," Mrs. Kendrick continued.

Nyx glimpsed back at the frail figure of a man standing beside the principal. He had not changed since the auditorium. If anything, he appeared weaker still. *Is this more than the grief over a lost childhood friend?* Nyx thought.

"Mr. Randolph revealed to us that he is a member of a consortium that has recently purchased the Palmer Inn overlooking Lynch Falls with the purpose of renovating it and re-opening it. Mr. Randolph said that it was near completion, and he offered to us the use of it Saturday night for the Sadie Hawkins dance."

"What a humanitarian," Westley said filled with acrimony.

"This'll be cool," said Nigel.

"Yeah, a haunted hotel on a cliff," said Nyx, feeling a lot like Scooby Doo. The concern about the synchronicity between the Scottish castle from Max's story and a deserted haunted hotel was just too much to ignore. "Nothing can go wrong with that idea."

Sliding his phone from his pocket, Nyx, with a press of a button, contacted Max.

"Max, I have news," Nyx said, in a whisper as the assembly was being dismissed, "and I need you to find out what you can on the Palmer Inn."

Chapter Twelve

...destined to repeat it

"And thus I clothe my naked villainy
With odd old ends stol'n out of holy writ
And seem a saint, when most I play the devil."

William Shakespeare
King Richard III

(I, iii, 336-338)

The Palmer Inn

Parking Lot

Friday, 10:30 AM

"This is going to be such fun," Billie said, putting the minivan into park.

Nyx peeked out through the windshield at the future site of the Parker's Point High School's Sadie Hawkins dance. Nyx had talked his mom into taking them to see the hotel prior to Saturday night. Billie had a meeting scheduled with her publisher over lunch, which would usually carry on into the afternoon, so she agreed to a morning excursion. Honestly, Billie was excited for the opportunity to see the location. As a writer, she was inspired by the majestic hotel and its colorful history.

Stepping out from the minivan, Nyx tried to take in everything that he could see.

"The hotel looks beautiful," Billie said. "Someone has certainly put some TLC into refurbishing this."

The recently re-poured concrete was solid beneath Nyx's feet as he moved about the empty parking lot. Though Nyx could not see it, the sound of Lynch Falls, water crashing and pounding on the rocks and river below, could be heard waffling through the serene country air. The hotel was a little over two miles northeast of Parker's Point creating the illusion of isolation and had been a popular escape in its day.

Westley, Nigel and Ariel piled out of the back of the minivan, and Ariel immediately started running around the parking lot, doing some energetic flips. She had been confined inside the vehicle for what seemed to her to be hours, though in actuality was only a few minutes. Ariel was never good when she was caged. This little bird had to fly free.

"I am sorry for that poor man's death," said Billie, "but I think this experience will be so much richer for the kids. This location is perfect for a dance."

Billie had been feeling much better since the conversation in Nyx's room, and her discovering that the man who claimed responsibility for vandalizing their home was now gone, eased her worries all the more. Nyx had his doubts about Rex Riley's guilt in this case, but he was happy to keep those doubts to himself for now.

"This doesn't look like a haunted hotel," Nigel said, with an air of disappointment.

"This hotel is not haunted," Billie said, "that's just an old wives' tale."

"But this *was* where Laura Truman was found," Nyx said, who had done his own research last night thanks to Google.

"Yes," Billie admitted, nodding toward Ariel, "but that's not something we need to be discussing right now."

Ariel did another series of flips across the lot, showing off the most athleticism ever displayed by a Grimm child.

"Ariel," her mom said, "do you want to see the falls?"

The young girl jumped into the air and rushed over to her mom. When they moved behind the hotel out of sight or earshot, Nyx turned to his brothers.

"This whole thing is just too familiar," Nyx said. "I don't like how this is lining up with the story Max told us."

"Who is Laura Truman?" Westley asked, not being involved in the research the night before.

"Nigel and I were researching this place last night. The hotel was booming until it was the site of the last unsolved homicide in Parker's Point."

"Yeah," Nigel said, "Laura Truman was class president and homecoming queen way back in the `80's"

"Whoa... ancient," said Westley.

"Yeah," Nigel replied.

"That is," Nyx continued, "until they discovered her body wrapped in bed linins and disposed of in the forest surrounding this place. According to Wikipedia, the case was never solved."

"Wikipedia? That's your source? You can't trust Wikipedia. Anyone can change those entries there," Westley balked.

"Wikipedia's great! I love Wikipedia," Nigel said. Nyx sometimes wondered if Nigel really believed what he said or if he took opposite positions just to wind Westley up.

"Either way, rumors of a spirit pacing the halls of the Palmer Inn and the negative publicity from the murder drove the owners to bankruptcy," Nyx finished.

"The Brothers Geek should solve that crime!" Nigel exclaimed. "How cool would that be?"

"Cold case at its finest," said Westley.

"We've got our hands full right now," said Nyx, once again striving to reign in his brothers.

"I'm not saying," said Nigel. "I'm just saying."

"It's not like the case is going anywhere," Westley added.

"That *would* be cool," Nyx finally agreed, "but now is not the time."

The brothers followed their mother and their sister around back, spying Billie, who was holding Ariel in her arms. The two of them were on the hotel's overhang watching the water plummeting over the edge. Ariel's bedazzled face displayed the amazement of childhood's marvel, pointing and gasping as the waterfall demonstrated nature's perceived invincibility.

"Wow, that's a long way down," Westley said, flabbergasted.

"Yes, it is," Billie said. "This is an amazing sight. I can't believe we haven't been here before now."

Nyx agreed. It was easy to lose yourself in the falling water, but Nyx weeded out the stunning visuals from his mind, his concentration like a laser searching for meaning or motive for Anthony Randolph to offer this locale for the dance. The series of coincidences that led to his offer was so contrived that there had to be more here than what Nyx was seeing.

"It's time we get going," said Billie, checking her watch. "I've got a meeting to get to."

So do I, Nyx thought.

Grimm Household

Living room

Friday, 12:10 PM

Nyx sat on the couch. With Ariel safely deposited at a last minute play date with her friend, Billie at her publisher's meeting, and Richard at work, the house was all Nyx's. It was the perfect chance to speak to Max.

Nyx hadn't seen Max since the day of the fire at Bright's Comix, but he had spoken to him a couple of times. The news that Rex Riley was dead eased Max's anxieties, but he shared Nyx's suspicions of Anthony Randolph. Nyx had hoped that Max would tell him that he was overreacting... that he was being paranoid. No such luck.

When the agent of the Guild of the Hidden arrived at the Grimm house, Nyx welcomed him inside. Not sure how to brew tea, Nyx offered Max some soda.

"Thank you, no," said Max, politely declining the offer. "There is an abundance of exposition to reveal."

"Before you start that," Nyx said, pulling out the accordion file and his iPod, he laid them on the table. "Can you pull fingerprints off items?"

"Of course. Why do you ask?"

"If Rex Riley was the person to break into our home, then he handled this file. It contained my RPG characters, and they wound up shredded on the floor. Only the Psybolt character sheet survived. I got Rex's prints on the iPod, and I'd like you to match them. This would prove he was here."

"I can do that Nyx," said Max cynically, "but Rex would have worn gloves to break in here. There is no conceivable way that someone like Rex Riley would leave a print at a crime scene."

"I agree," Nyx said, confusing Max with his apparently illogical thinking. "I would like to see if there are other prints on the file. Mine will be there, but if there are anyone else's... then that might help show that it was not Rex who broke in here."

"You believe it was not someone different?" Max asked.

"It doesn't feel right," Nyx said. "I don't know if you understand what I mean, but...."

"I do," Max said. He had learned to trust his intuition over the years. It had saved his life on many occasions. And he had always been impressed with Nyx's. "I will take care of this immediately. If there are other prints on here, we will find out to whom they belong."

"Hi Max," said Westley, as he and Nigel came out from their bedroom.

"Greetings, young Masters Grimm, it is indeed a pleasure to see you again," said Max in his true British accent.

"Hey," Nigel said, plopping down on the couch.

"I was about to tell Nyx about the information that I discovered," said Max.

"Cool," said Nigel.

"We're just in time then," said Westley, sitting, legs crossed, on the floor.

"Yes, I had my suspicions when you described to me about the albino who visited you in Prophesight, Nyx, but the tie in to *Psybolt* rang some bells for me. I went looking through Guild records on known mentalists from the last ten years."

"Wait a minute, mentalists?" said Westley. "Real mentalists?"

"Yes, there are real mentalists…and psychics… and mystics. It is their energy that encompasses the Prophesight. With Nyx's description, along with the fact that the vision did not speak to him, led me to Diego."

"San Diego?" Westley said.

"No… not San Diego, just Diego," Max said.

"Diego," said Nyx remembering, "I heard Rex say that name to Mr. Randolph when he was outside his office. He said something like he knew what Randolph had done to Diego, and he said something about Diego saving Randolph's life. I didn't understand any of that, but it didn't sound like two old friends catching up."

"Indeed," Max said. "Diego was an albino, but he was also mute and deaf. Of course, neither of those limitations made much difference for him. He spoke with his mind. Guild records indicated that he was quite powerful. He specialized in psionic surgery, and…"

"Hold on, Max," said Nyx, "what is psionic surgery?"

"It is a specific mental ability, very rare, that allows the mentalist to be able to mentally target specific masses, tumors and such much like a doctor would," Max answered. "Except where the doctor would use a scalpel as an instrument, the mentalist uses the power of the mind. A few of the faith healers around the world are actually psionic surgeons, just at lower level than Diego was."

"Was? What happened to Diego?" asked Nigel.

"Diego died a year ago after suffering a major brain injury a couple months prior. He passed away at a hospital in Dublin. His death took the staff by surprise. Several of them had said that they expected him to remain in a vegetative state for the rest of his life," Max said. "Interestingly enough, one of the major benefactors for the hospital was the Orion Group, which is the same group that purchased the Palmer Inn."

"No way!" said Nigel.

"That can't be," said Westley.

"Oh, but it is. Coincidences seem to abound through this case," Max said.

"Max, let me ask you this," Nyx said, rubbing his temples. "Would this psionic surgery leave any scars?"

"It would depend on the severity of the damage. It is possible," Max said, spotting Nyx rubbing his forehead. "Ah, I see what you're thinking."

"What?" Nigel said, not happy that he had missed something.

"Max, when you first told me about Anthony Randolph and what he did to those children in the castle in Scotland, you said that he had an inoperable brain tumor, right?"

"That's right," Max replied.

"And that he was collecting these children to drain them of their... life essence, like some kind of vampire, right?" Nyx said, realizing how ridiculous this would sound to those people who were outside the living room right now.

"Again, that is correct."

"And Anthony Randolph showed up here looking healthy and healed," Nyx said.

"Yes, he did," Max said, impressed with Nyx's thought process. "So you think Diego performed his psionic surgery on Anthony, curing him of his tumor."

"That wouldn't explain why Randolph is here," Westley said.

"Wouldn't it?" Nigel said. "Did you see Mr. Randolph today?"

"I did," Nyx said, staggered that Nigel had spotted Randolph's frailty. He thought Nigel was too busy arguing with Westley over Mr. Battle's pirate appearance.

"Randolph looked really sick," said Nigel. "I mean... really sick."

"Yes, he did," Nyx agreed.

"You mean...as if a brain tumor had returned?" Max said, finishing the train of thought that was streaming through the room.

"That would explain his motive. It would explain it all," said Nyx.

"That it would," said Max.

"So what do we do?" Nigel asked.

"I can't believe that Mr. Randolph thinks he can get away with kidnapping kids here in America... especially at a dance. How is that going to work?" Westley questioned.

"He may not be after just any kid," said Max. "He could be after only one kid...the Conduit."

"Me?" Nyx said.

"That would explain why Diego came to you, pointed at you, and lipped the word danger. He was telling you that you, as the Conduit, were in danger from Anthony Randolph," said Max.

"So," Westley said, "if you are right, then the entire dance is just a trap for Nyx. Nyx, you can't go."

"Oh, I'm going," said a defiant, almost cavalier Nyx. "If Anthony Randolph set this whole thing up to grab me, then it would be rude to not show up."

"I want to be Xander," said Nigel, out of nowhere.

"What?" Nyx said.

"Well, you're acting like this is an episode of *Buffy, the Vampire Slayer*. Nyx, you are Buffy, Max is clearly Giles… I don't want to be Willow, so in Buffy's Scooby gang, I want to be Xander."

"Come on, Nigel, this is serious," Nyx said.

"I know it is. This isn't a television show, but you sure seem to be acting like it is. If you are right, then this psycho wants you dead. He wants to drain you of … I don't know… whatever. He wants to keep himself alive by killing you," Nigel said, getting angrier with each passing word. The fear manifesting in his eyes was striking. "This isn't messing around with some high school kid who stole some money and framed a quarterback. This is life and death."

"What do you want me to do?" Nyx said. "I didn't ask to be the Conduit."

"Okay, *Buffy*," Nigel said.

"I'm with Nigel, Nyx," said Westley. "This is **way** too dangerous."

"And what do I do?" Nyx screamed in frustration. "If I don't show up at his little shindig, don't you think that he would try something else? Maybe he grabs someone I care about. What if he grabbed either of you? Heck, it worked for Julian. Do you think Randolph is above grabbing *Ariel*? Our family… our friends… none of them is safe while Randolph is plotting against me. I can't just stick my head in the sand."

The twins couldn't argue, no matter how badly they wanted to.

"I couldn't live with myself if Randolph hurt someone because he was coming after me," Nyx said, putting the exclamation mark on his argument.

"We could tell Dad," Westley said, quietly.

"We can't tell Dad. Why would he believe that the school's counselor wanted me dead? Oh, and by the way, I'm connected to some mystical, mental energy called the Prophesight, because I am the Conduit. No, that isn't going to work," said Nyx.

"What then?" said Nigel.

"I don't think I have a choice. I have to go to the dance and see what Randolph has planned and stop him," Nyx said.

"Just like that?" Nigel said.

"Yeah, just like that," he said.

"Except," Max said, interrupting the family drama between the boys, "we know he's planning something. We may not know exactly what it is, but knowledge is power. We can be ready for whatever he throws at you."

"Max could be a chaperone like Mom," said Nigel.

"That may not be the best idea, Nigel," said Max. "It may not be wise for someone with no connection to the school to show up out of the blue. Plus, Randolph knows who I am, so my presence out in the open would be a red flag for him. We don't want him to toss his plan aside. We want to catch him and stop him before he can bring his plan to fruition. It is a shame that the dance is at his property. If it were at the school, at least we would be on familiar ground."

"Lucky for him that they needed to move the dance," said Westley.

"Oh my God," Nyx said, though all three of the Grimm boys came to the conclusion at the same time. "Rex Riley's suicide was why they moved the dance, giving Randolph a tactical advantage."

"He killed him," said Westley and Nigel, in sync.

"He killed Riley," Nyx said, "and then he convinced Mrs. Kendrick to move the dance to his hotel. How long has he been planning this?"

"It does make some sick sense," said Max.

"What do you suggest we do, Max?" Nyx asked.

"I think we proceed as we planned. I will do my best in the shadows, in the background, where only you three know where I am," he said.

"Can you do that?" Westley asked. "I mean… no offense, but your leg…"

"No offense taken, Westley. My leg will not prevent me from doing what I can to aid you," Max answered. "I know what I can and cannot do. I can also provide a certain technological advantage."

The twins perked up immediately. Cool gadgets could help them push their fears to the back of their minds, giving them something to geek-out about. It was something to help them forget, if only for a short time, how petrified they were.

"What about the girls?" Nigel said. "Aren't we putting everybody else in danger going with them?"

"I don't think we have much of a choice. It's a Sadie Hawkins dance. The girls invited us, or else we wouldn't be going," said Nyx. "It's not like we can leave them ...*home*."

"Should we tell them about it?" Westley asked.

"No, the fewer people who know, the better," said Max.

Nyx had gone silent. As his brow wrinkled, Nyx was tormented by his own thoughts. Nyx's own words haunted him as a terrible notion had crossed his mind. His attempt to hide his distress was an epic failure.

"What is it, Nyx?" said Max, the first of the three to notice Nyx's deep and deliberate contemplation.

The depressing thought that had taken root in his mind would not leave his consciousness as his brothers detected his turmoil. Years of self-doubt and a negative self-image bolted back, attempting to smother the personal advances Nyx had made over the last few months like a candle in the wind.

"Nyx, are you alright?" asked Max again, suddenly extremely worried about the young boy, whose eyes stared blankly into space as if he were gazing into another time and place that he desperately wanted to alter. The realization hit him hard.

"*...or else we wouldn't be going,*" Nyx, at last, repeated, his words hanging on his tongue before finally, painfully revealing his inner misery. "I wouldn't be going to the dance had Helena not asked me. I was wondering why someone like her would ask someone like me me. Is this the reason? Could she be working for Randolph to make sure that I attended his trap?"

Finally putting words to the premise that had invaded his brain, Nyx knew that the invitation had not been given by choice. He knew that Helena was involved in this manipulation, and, no matter what the others had to say, Nyx Grimm had determined the truth. Helena Blood was a co-conspirator. It was the only thing that made sense.

"Are you alright?" Nigel asked, not usually the one to give pity which told Nyx one thing: Nigel believed the Nyx was right.

"I'm fine," said Nyx coldly, trying to get the image of the frightened, shivering girl out of his mind, replacing it with a cold, evil, Machiavellian jezebel. "It's time this ends... one way or another."

Chapter Thirteen

My Fair Lady

"Can we make this something good?
Cause it's all misunderstood"

-Daughtry

It's Not Over
Daughtry

The thin blue patterned tie kept the grey collar tight around Nyx's neck, as he stared toward the doorway, awaiting her arrival, hoping among hope that he could maintain his composure and his cool long enough to not blow everything.

However, the anger that had been swelling up inside Nyx since last night was dynamic, practically leaving a rotten aftertaste in his mouth. Nyx had to feign excitement as his mother fussed and fluffed him prior to dropping him off for their dinner.

Earlier that morning, Nyx had given Helena a call, pasting on his best fake sincerity, and asked her out to dinner before heading to the dance at the Palmer Inn. He wanted to be able to see what information or specific details that he could get out of her that might help him in the quest against Mr. Randolph. Nyx was convinced that Helena was an agent, for lack of a better term, of Randolph.

Nyx regretted making the date as soon as he hung up the phone. How could he get through the meal without revealing too much, or revealing everything, for that matter?   Nyx continued to take deep sips of the water on the table to attempt to wash the taste of bile from his mouth. Helena had made Nyx feel good about himself, confident, proud. The speculation about Helena's true motives has soured Nyx dramatically.

He removed his dark blazer, trying to avoid becoming too overheated. It would be hard enough to maintain his cool without being physically uncomfortable with his outfit. The tie was bad enough, as he tugged on it again, hoping to loosen the noose-like anchor.

Reaching into his blazer's inside pocket, Nyx removed the small ear piece that Max had provided to him earlier that day. He had given one to Nyx, Nigel and Westley and told them that they could communicate with each other and with him just by speaking normally. Westley and Nigel were in heaven, and they immediately began pretending to be Jack Bauer at CTU. Nyx slipped his into his pocket. He didn't want voices in his ear during his dinner with Helena. There were already too many voices of his own in his head without having to add the constant debates between the twins. Nyx needed some peace and quiet. So the communication unit went into his pants pocket for now.

Nyx had been replaying that Thursday morning over in his mind's eye, trying to find the spot that proved Helena was manipulating him. She had seemed sincerely frightened by the discovery of Rex Riley's dead body, but was she just acting? Was she acting like she did when she distracted Mrs. Kendrick for Nyx to get the fingerprints? Was she supposed to lead Nyx into that auditorium so they could *discover* the *suicidal* man? All of these thought were driving Nyx crazy, and they were only serving to amp up his stress levels. He tried not to think about it which only made him think about it more.

There had been a close call that morning with Nyx's father before he left for work.

"Nyx," Richard said, "I need to ask you a question."

"Yes, Dad," Nyx said, very much on edge.

"According to Mrs. Kendrick and Mr. Stanton, you said that you identified Riley's body for them. They said you called him *Rex Riley*."

"Yeah," Nyx said, not sure where he was going with that.

"How did you know his name?" Richard asked.

"I had read the suicide note," Nyx said, making his first mistake.

"But the suicide note was signed R. Riley, not *Rex* Riley. How did you know his first name?" Richard inquired.

Shoot, Nyx thought. He hadn't looked at the name closely as he had already known who the man was.

"Really?" Nyx said. "That's strange."

"So how did you know what his name was?" Richard pressed.

"I don't know. Maybe Mr. Randolph used his name when they were talking at his office, and it stuck in my head when I recognized the body," Nyx said, thinking that that would work. In fact, Nyx was even proud of himself coming up with the answer as quickly as he did.

"Okay, that makes sense," said Richard. "Thanks son for clearing that up."

Taking a quick glimpse at his phone, Nyx could see that it was nearly five o'clock, the time when Helena had agreed to meet him. Nyx had told her that they would enjoy a nice meal, and then his mother would pick them up and take them to the dance. He told Helena that he hoped she didn't mind sharing a ride with the twins, the Munroe sisters and his mother. She didn't.

A yawn escaped from his lips. The events that had unfolded last night played havoc with his sleep, finally dozing off around two. After a fitful night of tossing and turning, Nyx awoke anything but rested. Nyx was confident that adrenaline would kick in when he needed it.

The front door of the Olive Garden opened, and Nyx's breath was taken away by the vision walking inside the restaurant. Helena pinpointed Nyx in the busy eatery and, with an uncomfortable smile, moved toward the booth.

She didn't look anything like what Nyx had expected. He had pictured a black dress with a lot of lace, black fishnet stockings with stilettos and black make up. He even thought that there may have been a silver chain connecting the piercings.

Instead, Helena looked nothing like the Goth queen that she typically did. Though the piercings were still there, her jet black hair was pulled up on her head revealing her long, slender neck. A lone necklace with a single ruby draped around her throat. Her makeup was light, and only emphasized her natural features. She wore a low cut, shoulder-less blue gown. The bodice clung tightly to her, emphasizing each curve, down to her hips where the dress flared out into a floral pattered flexi skirt. As Helena approached, Nyx was sure that the skirt swayed like the waves of the ocean onto a sandy beach in the moonlight.

Helena was tentative, not looking to be comfortable with what she was wearing.

"Wow," Nyx said, standing from the booth. Helena's grateful smile beamed across the table.

"Hi," she said, holding her purse beneath her arm. "Have you been waiting long?"

"No...uh...no," stumbled Nyx. "I needed a few minutes away from the twins."

"I see," she said.

Looking at the dress, Nyx realized that the booth would not work.

"Um... we should probably move to a table," he said to the first waitress that moved past him. She laughed and led the young couple to a table. Nyx held out the chair, letting the angel sit first.

Why was I angry with her? Nyx thought.

"You look incredible, Helena," Nyx said, sitting back down. He hopped right up again. "I forgot my jacket."

Hurrying back to the booth, Nyx retrieved his blazer, slinging it over his arm. Taking a deep breath, Nyx tried to acclimate the new look with the cold-blooded girl he had been picturing the last twelve hours. It was so much easier for him to demonize her when she was dressed like a Goth.

Back at the table, Nyx draped his blazer over the back of his chair, and he sat down.

"My dress matches your tie," Helena said, sounding pleased.

"It does?" Nyx said. He had forgotten that he was wearing a tie. His entire preparation for this dinner was now out of the window. He **really** wished he hadn't set this up now.

"So, have you heard anything from your father about the guy in the auditorium?" Helena asked, trying to start a conversation.

"No, there's nothing," Nyx blurted, and then stopped, trying to be slicker. "I mean... they believe he committed suicide."

"Why did he choose to kill himself in our auditorium?" she asked. Nyx was confused why she kept asking about the case. *Didn't she already know this?* Nyx thought.

"I don't know. Maybe when Mr. Randolph told him he had to turn himself in, that was the final straw," Nyx said, thinking that sounded as good as anything.

"I don't like Mr. Randolph," Helena said. "He makes me feel like he is staring right through me, you know?"

"I do, actually," Nyx said.

"He's a creep. I don't know how he got a job as a counselor at a high school, but you couldn't pay me enough to take my problems to him," she said. "Why should I believe that he could help me, when he couldn't even help his friend?"

"What problems do you have?" Nyx asked.

"We all have problems, don't we? Some are worse than others, but we all have them," Helena said.

"I guess. Do you want to talk about anything?"

"Not really," she said. Nyx had hoped this would be easy, and Helena would turn out to be a talker. That didn't appear to be the case.

"Can I ask you a question?" Nyx asked.

"Why not," Helena said.

"What's with the tattoo?" Nyx said, looking at the spider that was now very out of place with Helena in this attire.

"It's not much of a story," Helena said, but the sadness in her voice told Nyx that she was not being honest about that.

"That's okay," he said.

"Okay, you asked for it," Helena started. "I got the tattoo when I was thirteen years old, on my thirteenth birthday, actually. My mother had just died six months before… cancer… and I was lonely and missing her so much."

"What about your father?"

"He tries, but he is too busy to really deal with me," she said. "So when I turned thirteen, I found a tattoo parlor of pretty low repute considering I was underage, and I had them give me my tat."

"Why a spider?" Nyx asked.

"Do you know the story of Arachne?"

"The Greek myth?" Nyx said.

"Yes, Arachne was turned into a spider by the goddess Athena."

"So you shall live to swing, to live now and forever, even to the last hanging creature of your kind," said Nyx, quoting the ending of the myth.

"You do know it," Helena said, smiling broadly. "My mom loved that story and would tell it to me all the time. She especially liked it because she was an amazing weaver herself, and she identified with Arachne. She was always sewing, weaving, crocheting, anything like that. She had great skill. I used to tease her about being a spider, and she would call me her little arachnid."

"What did your father say about the tattoo?"

"He flipped. He couldn't understand why I would do something like that to my body," she said, "and I think I had always reminded him of Mom. That was tough. Imagine looking every day at your daughter only to be reminded of your dead wife. That was when I started changing my look. I got some piercings, and dyed my hair black. I wanted him to see me, not Mom. And I would always have my tat to remind me of her."

"I'm sorry, that sounds rough," Nyx said.

"It has been better lately. This past summer my dad and I started to get to know each other again. We're actually in a pretty good place right now," Helena said. "He got me this dress."

"Well, we know that he has good taste," said Nyx, before he knew what was coming out of his mouth. He slapped himself across the forehead.

"That's a terrible line, Nyx," laughed Helena.

"I know," he said, "what do I know?"

Nyx didn't know what to think. Helena was forthcoming and open, and he thought she was being genuine with him. How could she be this wonderful and also be working for Randolph? Could she be that duplicitous?

"What about you?" Helena said. "I met your father, what about your mom?"

"Well, you're going to meet her in a little while, too," Nyx said. "She is a writer. She is working on her next book now."

"Anything I know?"

"Jacob Horror stuff," Nyx said.

"No way!" Helena gushed, sounding like Nigel. "Your mom is Mindy Mays?"

"That's her pen name," Nyx answered.

"Wow," she said, star struck. "I love her stuff. I can't wait to meet her."

"And she is about seven months pregnant," he said.

"Cool," said Helena. "Does she know if it's a boy or girl?"

"No. Mom and Dad like to be surprised. They never knew the sex of the babies before they came out," Nyx said, wishing he had said 'born' instead. "Mom thinks it is a boy, and Dad thinks it is a girl. They have a bet… winner gets to name the baby. I sure hope they do a better job than they did on the rest of us."

"You don't like Nyx?" Helena said.

"Why would I?"

"Because your name is one-of-a-kind. It's fascinating."

"Nyx Grimm… doesn't exactly roll off the tongue," Nyx joked.

"Nonsense, I won't listen to any more talk like that. You are lucky to have that name. You could have a last name like Blood. Helena Blood," she laughed. "Kind of creates a mental image, doesn't it?"

"I guess it does," Nyx said.

"So no more complaining about names, got it?" Helena demanded.

"Yes ma'am," Nyx said, saluting her.

"Now, if you would excuse me," she said, "I need to go *freshen up* before your mother comes to pick us up."

As Helena stood up, and headed for the ladies' room, Nyx was trying to wrap his mind around what was going on. He desperately wanted to forget everything he suspected and just believe that she was not involved. That she didn't know that Rex Riley was in the auditorium dead before she dragged him in there. That she was not working with Anthony Randolph to make sure Nyx came to the dance and into his clutches. That she could like him for him.

In the ladies' room, Helena checked to make sure that she was alone, and then she took out her phone from the glittering purse she held beneath her arm.

"Julian," she spoke. "It's Helena."

"How is our plan going, sweetheart?" Julian asked.

"I'm not feeling good about this, Julian," Helena said. "Nyx is a sweet boy. Why do we have to do this?"

"Don't go soft on me now, Helena," Julian said.

"But," she said.

"No buts," Julian interrupted, "we agreed. You don't want to let me down, now do you?"

"No," she said, disappointed.

"You just remember your part, Helena, and everything will turn out fine," Julian said.

Helena returned the phone to her purse. This was not the answer she had hoped to get. She wasn't sure what she had expected, but her heart wasn't in this any longer. But she didn't know what she could do.

Looking in the mirror in the ladies' room, Helena stared keenly at the reflection staring back at her. She searched for any sign that she was strong enough to do what had to be done. Turning her head to the side and using her hand, Helena blocked out the spider tattoo so she could no longer see it. She didn't want to see herself as herself anymore.

Chapter Fourteen

Behind the Curtain

"Gentlemen, let's broaden our minds... Lawrence."

-The Joker

Batman (1989)

The Palmer Inn

Front entrance

Saturday, 5:05 PM

The trip from the Olive Garden to Palmer Inn was somewhat uneventful and only moderately embarrassing. The twins, both dressed in ties, Westley's adorned with the Avengers while Nigel's pictured the Justice League of America, were on their best behavior, a nice switch. The Munroe sisters were smartly dressed, though they lacked the formal feel of Helena. Billie, full of the moment, was overjoyed with her boys and more than a few tears were shed and tons of pictures were taken.

Nyx escorted Helena from the van up to the front entrance of the inn. This magical point in time thrashed the realism Nyx had been feeling. Nyx was lost in the uncanny enchantment of the moment, wishing that it could last but aware that it wouldn't.

Inside the Palmer Inn, Nyx and Helena mooned at the breathtaking interior. The hotel was filled with wood shades and wooden structures, bringing to mind days of past. Signs posted led the Grimms and their dates to the ballroom. The DJ had started and, it could be heard that he was definitely earning his money.

Entering the ballroom, they were immediately taken by the design. They walked inside on an upper level, a small area with red carpeting. Silky red curtains ran alongside the walls along three sides of the room. There was a bar on this level that was set up with refreshments from the student council.

From this level, three sets of stairs led to a second level, with tables where students could sit and relax. This level formed a horseshoe around the bottom level, which was the large dance floor. A stage with an orchestra pit was included on the south end of the lowest level.

There was already a packed dance floor as the DJ had set up in the south corner just off the band pit, and he was blaring Lady Gaga's *Bad Romance*.

"Come on, Nyx," Helena said, grabbing him by the hand, "I love this song."

Pulling him behind her, the pair scaled the steps toward the bottom level, and they found their way out onto the dance floor. Nearly shoulder to shoulder with their peers, Helena threw herself into the rhythm of the music, swaying back and forth in perfect time. Nyx, hardly skilled at dancing, just tried his best not to stand out among the mass of students. Ideal situation to him was for no one to realize that he was even there... to be lost in the crowd. He'd done it for years in hallways, just not in a freestyle social setting such as this.

"Nyx, Westley, Nigel, systems check."

Despite not being anywhere in sight, Max's voice in Nyx's head was clear as could be despite the pounding music. Turning his head away from Helena, Nyx covered his mouth.

"I hear you Max," said Nyx, quickly.

"Copy that," Nigel said, his voice also ringing through Nyx's head.

"Go ahead, CTU," Westley said, the fantasy playing through his head.

Nyx could not see his brothers, but he could hear them as clearly as if they were standing right beside him. The technology that Max had provided was amazing. When this idea originally was brought up, Nyx was sure that he would be hearing Nigel and Westley's constant chatter in his head for the entire evening. He had braced himself for their steadfast arguments. However he did not hear anything of the sort. The communication devices only activated when they were talking to Max or to one another. Nyx desperately wanted to know how the devices worked, but he fought back the curiosity knowing that any distractions could be a disaster.

"Nyx, I was able to pull other prints besides yours off the file. They weren't Riley's fingerprints either. As I expected, there was no sign of Riley's prints on the file. That does not clear him, but," Max said.

"No one else would have touched that file," said Nyx. "That would make me wonder where those prints came from."

"And there were plenty of them," Max continued. "This person wasn't worried about leaving fingerprints, in fact, this person may not have even thought about it. That makes me think that this is an amateur."

"Julian?" Nyx asked.

"No, it's not Julian. His prints are on file at the police station, and I was able to compare them. They did not match."

Nyx was impressed with Max's ability to access police files. He wondered if Max had hacker skills like Nigel.

"I will continue to try to find a match to the prints while you are there, Nyx," Max said.

"What are you doing, Nyx?" Helena asked, noticing that Nyx had stopped *dancing* and appeared to be talking to himself.

"Oh… sorry, I just remembered something that I need to get done tomorrow," Nyx quickly covered. "It's no big deal."

"Alright, because tomorrow doesn't matter right now," Helena said.

As Lady Gaga sang her final ga ga ooh-la-las, out of the corner of his eye, Nyx identified Julian peeking from behind a curtain on the floor level. Julian ducked back behind the red silk curtain into a back room.

"By request," the DJ said across the microphone, "here's a slow song… by Foreigner."

> *I got to take a little time*
> *A little time to think things over*
> *I better read between the lines*
> *In case I need it when I'm older*

Helena yanked Nyx close to her and into an embrace. Her eyes closed as they danced slowly, and she melodiously began to sing along.

"*Now this mountain I must climb feels like the world upon my shoulders,*" she sang.

"You have a beautiful voice," Nyx said while trying to make sure that he did not step on Helena's feet, thus breaking the mood.

"Thanks," she said, suddenly a little shy, before returning to the song. "*In my life, there's been heartache and pain. I don't know if I can face it again.*"

As Helena belted out the Foreigner lyrics, Nyx noticed that Mr. Randolph was on the stage looking at something. Nyx could not tell what he was doing. Randolph was still very ragged, and he kept glancing over to the DJ with contempt and an irritated expression, rubbing his head.

Helenahad grown quiet as she continued to sway to the soft music. Her eyes had become watery, tearing up for no apparent reason. Nyx wasn't sure if this was in reaction to the song or something else. The smile on her face was gone, replaced by a rueful frown as she tightened her grip on the embrace.

The DJ transitioned immediately from the soft sound of *I Want To*

Know What Love Is into the Black Eyed Peas' *I Gotta Feeling*. The beats drove Randolph quickly from the stage, but Nyx did not notice as his hands were abruptly full.

"I-I can't… do this anymore," Helena sobbed, pulling out of the clench. "I'm so sorry, Nyx."

Helena turned to run for the stairs, ascending them as rapidly as her outfit would permit.

"Helena?" Nyx yelled, shocked. The sudden reversal of the evening's fortunes confounded Nyx. Frozen in place, Nyx did not know what to do. This was so far outside his area of expertise… or comfort, for that matter.

"Dude, go after her."

Shane Dietz, the backup quarterback on the Parker's Point Lions, had observed the entire meltdown. Shane stood with his arm enveloping the smallish girl he was with.

"Go on, Nyx, she needs you. I know you've got it in you," said Shane, who had apparently become Nyx's own personal Qui-Gon Jinn. "You've proven that."

With a silent acknowledgment to Shane, Nyx proceeded to pursue his date off the dance floor. He had no idea what he was going to do if he caught up to her, but he would improvise.

Helena fled to the second level and found a table farthest from the stairs. She had hoped to exit the Palmer Inn completely, but there had been several senior couples on their way down to the dance floor providing a barrier to her escape and forcing a detour.

As Nyx approached, he could tell Helena was an emotional train wreck. She buried her face in her arms on the table as her gentle weeping dissolved into the boom of the rock and roll.

"Helena, what's wrong?" Nyx asked, sliding unnoticed into the chair beside her, Helena did not respond. She couldn't find the words to explain the guilt eating away at her, and she was afraid what would happen if she made eye contact with him. Nyx reached his hand over and softly touched her arm, which only made her feel worse.

Finally, with wet eyes averted, Helena stared out at the teenagers below and their enjoyment of their carefree ritual. It was an instant Helena wanted to freeze in time, a time before she joined in a cruel scheme to hurt a young boy she didn't know. It was so much easier before she had known him, when he was just a face in the crowd. Part of her wished that she could return to that time. Anything to avoid the pain and betrayal she knew would be written on his face when the truth was finally exposed.

"I'm sorry, Nyx," she said, not wanting to expand on the thought. Helena knew that she had no choice, and she continued, "I have to tell you something."

"I know already," Nyx said, ending the charade.

"What?" a stunned Helena said, stealing a glance at Nyx.

"I know why you asked me to the dance," Nyx said.

"You... do?" The tremor in her voice exposed the fear and vulnerability she felt. The disappointment she saw was worse than she ever expected or believed possible.

"Yes," Nyx said, emotionless. He had had time to own the anger, to process the situation and work his way through it. A pleasant evening to this point helped, but Nyx knew it was just a matter of time before everything blew up in his face.

"How... did you find out?" Helena stuttered.

"I figured it out," Nyx said. "It didn't take much to realize why someone as beautiful as you would want to spend time with someone like me."

"Don't say that," she said, objecting to Nyx's diminishing himself.

"Why not? It's true," Nyx said, keeping his cool. He was playing this close to his vest as the young geek ran specific words through his mind. He would not give her the satisfaction. "So, I'm here. You did your job and got me to the dance. When do I find out why Randolph wants me here?"

"Wh-what?" Helena sputtered, questioning whether she had heard Nyx correctly.

"You don't have to pretend anymore, Helena," Nyx said. "I know the truth."

"What do you think you know?" she asked.

"Mr. Randolph wanted me at this dance for some warped reason, and you are working with him to make sure I attended," Nyx said. "I just don't know why."

"Mr. Randolph?" Helena was confused. "I'm not working with Mr. Randolph."

"You can stop now," Nyx said, becoming angry that Helena continued with her pretense. "I'm here. I'm not going anywhere until this is over."

"Nyx," Helena said, "you're wrong. That's not true."

"If that's not true," puzzled Nyx, "then exactly what is going on here? Why are you so upset?"

Helena paused to gain her composure once again. She was dreading this. She wished that she had never agreed to do this. Hindsight being 20/20, Helena would have done everything differently since the day that she met him.

"It was Julian," she said, with a final blurt. It was out in the open now.

"Julian?" Nyx said, giving Helena his undivided attention.

"I had been seeing Julian secretly for a few weeks. He said it was better that way, with the trouble he was in," she said. "He told me about his mother, and how he felt deserted by her. She always puts her patients first, and that is difficult for him. I felt bad for him."

"Julian?" Nyx repeated, wrapping his head around it. "He uses the mother card as an excuse for his bad actions."

Nyx realized that Helena had traits and situations in common with Julian that he could manipulate. Her mother issues led to her having a tattoo on her neck and face so her father wouldn't look at her and see her mother. Nyx could guess that Julian played on those emotions to get Helena to do what he wanted.

"Then he came to me with a plan," she said. "He wanted me to get close to you and get you invested in a relationship, and then we would pull the rug out from under you. He wanted to make you suffer for betraying him,"

"Betraying him?" spat Nyx. "He's delusional, you know. Betraying him… you don't believe that I betrayed him, do you?"

"Not now," she said, dropping her head, "but he was convincing."

"So…"

"The dance came up, and we agreed that this was a perfect chance to put our plan into effect," she said.

"Helena, I need you to think hard, and I need you to tell me the truth. Whose idea was the dance?"

Helena thought back to the formation of the plan, and she said, "Well, I guess Julian brought it up, first."

"See… you are working with Mr. Randolph, even if you don't know. Julian is working with Randolph, and so are you."

"I don't understand," she said.

"I wouldn't expect you to," Nyx said. "I'm not sure I understand it completely."

"I was supposed to get close to you, but I didn't expect to find what I did. I didn't think that I would find such a wonderful person. I really like you, Nyx. This hasn't been an act," said Helena. "You made it easy."

"So what *has* been an act? I really believed you were afraid when we found Rex's dead body. How long did you know he was there?"

"What? I was just as surprised as you were when we found him. Seeing you deal with him was the first time I saw the real you." she said, narrowing her eyes. "What are you thinking? You don't think Julian had something to do with his death."

"Not Julian, necessarily, but Randolph, yes," Nyx said.

"That's crazy, Nyx. Why would Mr. Randolph be involved in a man's death?" Nyx couldn't tell if Helena was acting now or was legitimately confused.

"How can I believe you?" Nyx said. "You've been lying to me the whole time."

"Not the whole time," she said. "Yes, I went into this with less than noble motives, but the time we spent together was true. I enjoyed spending time with you, and you are the reason that I am questioning my role in this."

"Whatever," he said.

"Not whatever, Nyx. I am so sorry that I did this, and I don't expect that you'll be able to forgive me, but don't believe for one minute that you are less because of who you are or what I did. You are so special... Do you remember when I asked you to this dance in the first place?"

"In the cafeteria," Nyx said.

"Yes, do you remember what I said then?"

"You called me a hero," Nyx said.

"That's right. And I was right then. You are a hero. You are brave and honest, and I feel ashamed by what I tried to do to you." Helena stopped and put her head back down. "I'm sorry."

Nyx held himself back as he wanted to move over to her to comfort her. Either way, she was involved in this, and it was time for this to be over. He stood from the table ready to move things along.

"Where are you going?" Helena asked between tears.

"This ends now," he said, full of determination and conviction. "I guess I have to go see Julian."

Chapter Fifteen

A Deadly Twist

"I keep telling you, you listen to me more, you live longer."

-Short Round
Indiana Jones and the Temple of Doom

Sadie Hawkins Dance

The Palmer Inn

Saturday, 5:45 PM

Nyx knew where he was going. He had seen Julian lurking around earlier while he and Helena danced. He was cowardly hiding behind the red curtain like the Great and Powerful Oz, only with less of an altruistic spirit. Julian was hiding hoping the world did not see his true face, but Nyx was not going to allow that to continue. Julian's delusion needed to come to a close. It was time to pull back the curtain.

With each step down to the dance floor, Nyx's determination grew greater. Helena had tried to talk him out of a confrontation here, but Nyx's mind was made up, and he left the sobbing girl alone at the table. He didn't have time to worry about her feelings of guilt over her involvement in this mess. If history told him anything, Anthony Randolph was a danger. Nyx understood that this was life and death, and he could not afford any dangling holes in the plot.

Crossing the dance floor was going to be a challenge for Nyx. He did not have the mass required to proceed to the back room, but Nyx had a solution. A quick tap on Shane Dietz's shoulder and a request led to an augmented blocker leading the way through the crowd for the diminutive geek. Nyx saluted his friend, and he turned to the curtain where he had seen Julian before. A deep breath cleared the excess doubt from his courage and Nyx pressed on.

Flipping the curtain aside, Nyx stepped into the hallway behind it. A slight crack of light beneath a door had signaled him where he needed to go. Slowly moving through the darkened pathway, Nyx arrived at the closed door. Placing his ear against the door, Nyx strained to hear what was happening within the room. The music from the dance was still too loud to hear anything of substance from the room, so Nyx reached for the doorknob.

God hates a coward, Nyx thought, as he twisted the knob.

The door opened easily, and Nyx cautiously made his way inside.

Julian, with his back to the door, sat facing a vanity mirror against the back wall of the room, elbows on the table, both of his hands grasping his head. Julian was slouched with his eyes closed.

"Alright Julian, I'm here now," Nyx said. "What's going on here?"

Julian did not respond to Nyx. He did not even flinch. Nyx worried that he wasn't even breathing, but the slight inhale and exhale of his chest could be seen.

"Julian? What are you trying to pull?"

"I'm not trying to pull anything, Nyx," said Julian, slowly, deliberately. "It's Anthony Randolph."

"Yeah, I know about Randolph," Nyx said, "but I'm talking about **you** right now."

Julian turned in the chair and made a connection with his former friend. His face was a mask of a nightmare from which someone had just awoken.

"Nyx, you don't understand. It's Randolph, he's after you. You've got to get out of here," Julian said.

"I'm not going anywhere, Julian, and you can knock off the act. It's not going to work. I am on to you."

"Nyx," Julian said, standing up and nearly falling down. His legs wobbled as he tried to steady himself. "This isn't about me. This has never been about me. This has always been about you."

"Helena told me the truth. She told me that you planned to make me fall for her, and then rip her away. Well, it's not going to work. You misjudged her level of cruelty, Julian. She didn't want to hurt me like that, and she told me the truth. But we both know the real reason was just to draw me to the dance," Nyx said.

"Helena is just a pawn. So am I. It's Randolph. He's after you," said Julian.

"Why is that?" Nyx said, hoping that Julian would continue revealing information like a monologuing villain.

"Because he knows that you are the Conduit," Julian said.

"And so this was a perfect chance for you to jump aboard with your whacked plan of revenge. All this because I stopped you from destroying a man's life?"

"You're not listening to me," Julian said, desperation sneaking into his words. "Randolph wants you, and he is really dangerous."

"I know how dangerous he is," Nyx said.

"No you don't. He can make people do things… things they wouldn't do before," said Julian.

"Hold on," Nyx responded with contempt, catching Julian's point. "So are you saying that Mr. Randolph made you do the things that you did against your will?"

"No," Julian said, "I made my mistakes with Penny and Noah, and I will take the blame for them. But Nyx, did you ever think that I was capable of grabbing Westley and hurting him?"

"No, I didn't know what you were capable of," Nyx replied.

"Did you realize that none of that happened until after Anthony Randolph showed up at Parker's Point High School? After he arrived, I grabbed Westley, threatened you, became angry all the time, manipulated Helena and sent her to you. And I did all of that because of Penny Harris? Does that make sense?"

"You are delusional," Nyx said, wondering if Julian had finally gone off the deep end.

"You don't believe me," Julian said. "I don't blame you. I wouldn't believe me either. It sounds delusional, but Anthony Randolph can make people do things that they don't want to do. Just ask Nigel and Westley."

"What?" Nyx exclaimed.

"Randolph made Westley ransack your living room and paint that graffiti on your wall," Julian said.

"Westley? Are you nuts? Westley didn't wreck our living room," said Nyx defiantly. "I've never heard such a ridiculous story."

"Randolph made him do it. Westley may not even remember doing it. Didn't it seem odd to you that Westley was home alone and never heard someone messing up your house?"

"Why would Westley do that? You're speaking gibberish," Nyx said.

"I'm not," Julian said. "I'm finally free."

"I don't believe you," said Nyx.

"And why was it so important to Westley to come to this dance? He badgered Nigel constantly, didn't he? And Nigel changed his tune about coming tonight rather abruptly after he was… where?"

Nyx paused and retraced the events. He said, "In Mr. Randolph's office."

"Right," Julian said. "Randolph would work over Westley every morning while you and Nigel worked on the office computers, and he would find reasons to see Nigel. Stupid reasons like needing help on the computers would be all he'd need."

Nyx turned away from Julian, but he kept him in sight out of the corner of his eye.

"Max," Nyx said, "check those fingerprints against Westley's, would you please? Dad had all of our fingerprints on file at the police station just in case something happened so the prints should be as accessible as Julian's were."

"Why," said Max.

"I just need to check on something," Nyx said, turning back to Julian.

"So you came tonight with backup? Good, because I'm afraid you are going to need it," Julian said.

"Why don't you tell me, Julian, because you seem to be the one in the know. Why does Anthony Randolph want me dead?"

"Dead? He doesn't want you dead. He needs you. He wants to control you," said Julian.

"He wants to control me? How is that going to work?" Nyx said.

"I told you, he can make people do things they don't want to do."

"What is his plan then? Why was it so important that I come to this dance?"

"Nyx," interrupted Max. Nyx turned away from Julian again to listen to the voice in his head.

"Yes, Max," said Nyx.

"You were right. The fingerprints belonged to Westley," said Max.

"I'll get back to you in a second, Max," Nyx said. He knew that Westley had lied to him. Westley had touched the file. *Could this be true,* Nyx thought.

"Well, what did he say?" Julian said.

"It doesn't matter," said Nyx, his non-answer telling Julian what he wanted to know. "Before I was interrupted, you were going to tell me why it was so blasted important for me to be at this dance."

"You didn't have to be here," said Julian. "If you were here, that would be fine to him, but his plan did not hinge on you being here."

"Wait, I don't understand. You said that he was after me. That he wanted to control me, not kill me. So what is going on here? If he didn't want me here, why go to all the trouble of getting the twins…" Nyx stopped. "He wanted the twins here?"

"Yes," said Julian.

"Why?"

"Randolph wanted you broken. He wanted you to have no fight left in you. He wanted you to feel the pain that he felt as a youth," Julian said.

"What are you talking about?" Nyx questioned.

"When Randolph was a young boy, he had two brothers who died in a car bomb on a crowded street in Belfast. It was one of the greatest regrets of his life. He knew that feeling of grief and loss was devastating and debilitating, and that is the way he wants you to be," Julian said, "like a broken slave that had been beaten down by his master's whip."

"So what you are telling me, Julian, is that Randolph isn't after me tonight," Nyx started.

"He's after the twins," Julian finished.

Placing his hands on his earpiece, Nyx said, "Westley, Nigel... you guys need to get out of here. Go to the meeting point with Max right now."

There was no response.

"Nigel! Westley! Enough of the games guys, you need to answer me right now!" Nyx exclaimed, getting more worried. "Max, are you there?"

"Yes, Nyx," he said.

"Randolph's after the twins, and they won't respond to me. Is there something wrong with their ear pieces?"

Nyx was beginning to panic. What had he brought the twins into?

"They appear to be active, Nyx," Max replied, "but they are not responding to me either. Maybe they took them out for some reason."

Nyx lunged at Julian, grabbing him by his shirt and pulling him closer, showing more strength than he ever thought he had possessed. The fury filled strength helped Nyx pin Julian against the wall.

"What is he planning on doing to them, Julian!" screamed Nyx.

"I don't know," he said. "I just know that he planned on it happening tonight."

"And he killed Rex Riley to make sure that the school would agree to move this dance to his hotel, right?" Nyx exclaimed.

"Yes, well... he made Rex kill himself," said Julian.

"He made Rex kill himself? He's capable of something like that? How?"

"I think you know," said Julian. "He's been leaving hints to you since this whole thing started."

Psybolt, Nyx thought.

"Mind control?" Nyx said. "If he's that powerful, then what does he need the twins here for? Couldn't he have just had them kill themselves like he did to Riley?"

"He wanted you to feel the pain that he felt. The same pain," Julian said.

The tension was broken by the announcement of the DJ over the loudspeaker, slightly muffled in the back room.

"We would like Nigel and Westley Grimm to come to the stage please," the DJ's voice sliced through the dance. Nyx stared at Julian, whose face was twisted in worry.

"No, it can't be," said Nyx, thinking about two young boys dying in a car bomb on the crowded Belfast street.*How would Anthony Randolph simulate that same kind of terrorism on the shores of this country?* Nyx was afraid he knew.

"Go!" Julian yelled.

Nyx released Julian's shirt and tore from the backroom faster than he had ever moved before. His panic fueled muscles stretched and strained as Nyx reached the red curtain. Busting through, he saw his brothers both walking up on the stage. Nyx yelled, but the music being played drowned out his screams. The dance floor was swamped with students from the school, and, even with a blocker, Nyx would not be able to wade his way through the pack in time.

The accelerated pounding in his chest reverberated across him, blocking out the surrounding environment. With each breath, the world around Nyx moved in slow motion as he watched each step his brothers took toward impending doom. Westley and Nigel moved closer to the exact spot Randolph had been examining earlier.

Quickly scanning the area, Nyx saw the stage entrance behind the DJ's booth. This would be the only chance Nyx would have, and it was a slim one indeed.

Skirting to the peripherals of the dance floor, Nyx dashed, avoiding all obstructions like an Olympic skier on a gold medal slalom run. The pumping, angst-induced adrenaline spurred his muscles to feats of physical exertion unforeseen before as he bounded up the stairs to the stage. Without noticing, Nyx flashed past Billie.

"Nyx?" Billie said to the blur that rushed toward the open stage. The sounds did not register with Nyx as his senses had fixated completely on just one goal.

He streaked across the stage, barreling into Westley and Nigel, a hand in both of their backs. With his built-up momentum and with every ounce of strength he could muster, Nyx sent the twins shooting from the stage like stuntmen from *The A-Team*. Westley and Nigel crashed into the padded chairs of the orchestra pit with a thud. The gasp of the dumbfounded audience who witnessed the aggression spread across the dance floor, replaced immediately by whispers debating the brotherly motive.

The DJ was stunned by the hit and run attack on the two helpless freshmen boys by the kid with the glasses. He turned and ran for the stairs to go down to see if he could help the victims.

In a split second, Nyx readied himself to leap from the stage and follow his brothers into the relative safety of the band pit. Images of Bruce Willis leaping from the top of the Nakatomi Plaza with a fire hose tied around his waist zoomed through his head when a voice stopped him in his tracks.

"*Nyx Edgar Grimm*, what in God's name are you doing?" Billie said, running across the stage toward her eldest son, who she believed had completely lost his mind.

"Get out of here, Mom!" Nyx screamed, meeting her near the edge of the stage.

BOOM

Chapter Sixteen

Trapped

"Oh, so that's what an invisible barrier looks like."

-Fidgit

Time Bandits

Sadie Hawkins Dance

The Palmer Inn's Dance Floor

Saturday, 6:01 PM

Screams and shrieks abounded as the students from Parker's Point High School dodged flying debris from the massive explosion that had consumed the stage in a ball of fire and smoke.

Covered in ash and splinters, Nigel coughed, trying to clear his lungs of the smoke. He had hit his head on one of the chairs when Nyx had shoved him from the stage, and he was just now regaining his consciousness.

"Westley," Nigel said between coughs, "where are you?"

Groaning, Westley picked himself up from behind the seat where he had ducked as the explosion rocked the room. He held his left arm against his chest. He knew it was broken, but the pain was unimportant. This pain could wait.

"Yeah," he replied to his twin, "I'm okay."

"What happened?" Nigel asked, trying to clear the cobwebs.

"There… was an explosion," said Westley. "The stage blew up… right where we would have been standing if…"

Westley began frantically searching around the area, moving rubble aside.

"Nyx!" he began to yell. "Nyx! Where are you?"

The only response to Westley's cries was silence. The realization struck Nigel harder than the fall.

"Nyx!" Nigel screamed, joining his brother in the physical search around the area.

"Oh," Westley said, reaching into his pocket and grabbing Max's communication device. Returning it to his ear, Westley yelled, "Nyx… Nyx… come in, Nyx."

"Westley," Max said, responding to the young boy's desperate call. "Where have you been? What happened in there?"

"Max? There was an explosion," Westley said, gaining a semblance of calm at hearing the British accent.

"Good lord… is everyone alright?" Max asked.

"We can't find Nyx," he answered, bravely trying to hold back the tears. "You've got to help us."

"Kids are running out the door. I'll be there as soon as I can," Max said. "Try to hold on and remain calm."

The teachers and other chaperones were trying to maintain control while evacuation procedures were underway. The screams continued from the frightened youth as they filed to freedom. Each scream sent another chill down Westley's back at the deadly prospects.

Above the dance floor, Helena could not remove her eyes from the scene that unfolded before her. She had watched Nyx as he entered the room below her. She had seen him come out again, noticeably anxious and spooked. She watched his mad rush to the stage and his bizarre push of his brothers. The confusion drained away with the unexpected blast, and she had affixed her gaze, maintaining her surveillance since. The jolt did not bring tears. Instead, it brought disbelief as Helena prayed that Nyx had survived, and that she had not played a role in this tragedy.

Spreading around the ballroom, the smoke created an illusion of a fog swept morning with visibility to challenge all but those with superior vision. Those remaining strained to determine the fate of the unfortunate student near the epicenter of the blast.

The stage floor was gone, replaced by a massive crater surrounded by flames and damage. Because the nearby curtains threatened to send the entire structure into an uncontrollable inferno, a battalion of do-gooders, led by Shane and Noah, attempted to prevent the flames from spreading from the isolated area. Beating the fire back, the assembled students made progress versus the fire tetrahedron, but they dared not celebrate their success… not in the face of the unresolved result of the bombing.

Already not a strong point for them, Westley and Nigel were anything but patient as they tried to get close to the hole. Neither boy had realized yet that their mother was among the missing. They feared that their brother had sacrificed himself for them, and that thought was almost too much for them to stand.

"Nigel, Westley," Max said, dragging his damaged leg through the chaos. The twins rushed over to him, a lantern of optimism in the darkness of realism, a Utopian minute amidst this dystopian hour.

"We can't find Nyx," Westley said, almost hysterical. Max wrapped his arms around the boys, trying to comfort them. Max noticed the absence of Billie Grimm immediately, but he realized these already distraught boys did not need another worry loaded upon them.

"Relax, boys," Max said, "Nyx will be fine. You know he is a very capable young man. And he is the Conduit… if anything would have happened to him, I'd know."

Max lied. He prayed that it was only a little white lie, but there was no mystical or magical way for Max to know if something had happened to Nyx. Max's fictitious misstatement had the desire effect as the twins breathed a sigh of relief and regained their equilibrium.

"We tried to contact you guys over the coms, but you didn't respond. What happened?"

"We took them out," Nigel said.

"You took them out?" mimicked Max. "Why did you do that?"

"We were supposed to," Nigel said, without elaboration.

"Yes," Westley agreed, "we were supposed to take them out."

"Who told you to take them out?" Max questioned.

Westley and Nigel looked at each other as if they expected the other one to know the answer. When neither offered an explanation, puzzlement breached the twins' faculties.

"That's not important now," Max said, having seen examples like this before. "Now we have to find your brother."

Examining the stage from the dance floor, Max was not overcome with confidence. With the path to the stage still blocked, Max decided the best hope was the technology.

"Nyx, it's Max. Nyx, come in," Max said, repeated that line into his com. "Bloody 'ell, Nyx, answer me!"

Haze. Fog. Pandemonium. An explosion. Flames. Smoke. Cloudiness. Miasmatic. Smooth slide.

Nyx

Rush of air against his skin. Dizziness. The abrupt smack of flesh against rock.

It's Max.

The warm flow of blood past his chin. Mustiness. Muddled. Blur.

Bloody 'ell, Nyx

Pain. Choppy breath. Hard. What?

      …answer me.

"Max?"

"Nyx!" an excited Max said, finally receiving confirmation that the young geek had survived the explosion. The twins anxiously hurried to Max's side. "Are you alright? Where are you?"

"Can't... see," Nyx muttered. "Glasses?"

Nyx forced himself to his hands and knees and, between pain-filled gasps of air, began randomly tapping the damp ground in search of his glasses. Reaching up to his face, Nyx wiped his hand across his nose and mouth. Still dazed, the red juice loomed on his fingers.

"I'm bleeding," Nyx said.

"Are you alright?" Max said.

"What happened, Max?" Nyx spit out as he resumed his pell-mell search.

"There was an explosion," Max said.

"Explosion?" Nyx said, the word halting his hunt. Flashes of recollection flicker in Nyx's head like satellite television during a heavy thunderstorm. "Nigel? Westley?"

"They are fine," said Max.

"Mom!" Nyx said, the last seconds on the stage finally finding their way back to Nyx. He continued to call out to his mother as his search for his glasses all at once took on more meaning. "Max, is Mom there with you?"

"No, Nyx," Max said, seeing the twins realize the fact that their mother was not there.

"Mom! Mom!" The screams returned in Nyx's own voice. The echo did not stop him. Neither did Max's attempts to calm him down with soothing words. Cognizance was gradually returning to Nyx through the dream state he had been lost in, and the recognition of what had happened and its potential results were terrifying.

Finally finding his glasses, Nyx forced the bent frames into place, and, ignoring the pain that slashed through his body, he struggled to his feet.

"Max, I'm in a cave," Nyx said, looking around. The sound of running water drew his attention. "Mom!"

Billie Grimm laid, unmoving, on her back with her lower body in the small stream that trickled through the underground shaft. Nyx pulled her drenched physique from the water and supported her against his chest.

"Mom?" Nyx said softly, "It's okay. You're okay. Please be okay."

As Nyx cradled his mother in an unknown cave, Julian pushed aside the red curtain and walked out to the dance floor. After hearing the massive explosion and the subsequent panic, Julian was afraid to leave the back room. He wanted to avoid seeing the scene for which he was at least partially responsible, but his morbid curiosity won out.

Moving toward the stage, Julian could see Max and the twins trying to get closer to the gaping hole where the stage once was.

"You did this!"

The feral scream from behind Julian stunned him as Helena began pounding on his chest with ferocity Julian had not experienced before.

"Is this enough for you?" she screamed. "Was this enough?"

"Helena, I…" Julian began, trying to stop the barrage of blows from the wild girl. With a sharp slap across his face, Julian grabbed Helena's arms and shoved her to the ground.

"I'm sorry, Helena," said Julian, immediately regretful for his physical action. He reached his hand out to help her up, but Julian never had a chance to see if she would have accepted it.

"Bastard!"

Nigel's caterwaul preceded him projecting himself like a spear, tackling the Uber Geek. The smallish freshman's frenetic strikes rained down upon Julian with a righteous wrath. Julian covered his head with his arms as Nigel, straddling his one-time idol, maintained the storm of shots at the helpless foe.

"I – didn't want this!" Julian exclaimed.

Nigel was not hearing anything. The berserker fury fueled the savage assault and mutated the puny, undersized freshman into an unstoppable juggernaut of retribution. The fear pounded out of Nigel, manifesting in violence toward a single target.

"That's enough, Nigel," said Westley, pulling his twin off the hapless Julian while trying to protect his own broken left arm. "He's not worth it."

"Why, Julian?" yelled Nigel, the anger directed solely at the Uber Geek.

"I didn't want this," Julian said, holding his head. "It was Randolph."

"It was you!" Nigel screamed. "You're not getting out of this!"

"Our mother was on that stage," Westley said, quietly.

"No," Julian said.

"Yes!" Nigel exclaimed. "And I swear… if anything has happened to her…"

"Come on, Nigel," interrupted Westley, with his right arm shrouding Nigel. He pulled back on his twin. "Let's get back to work."

"Thanks, Westley," said Nigel.

"Boy, you sure Hulked up on him, dude," Westley said.

"Yeah, I don't know where that came from," Nigel said.

Julian sat on the dance floor nursing his wounds and bruises from the dual onslaughts, and he glanced around the chaos he had wrought. Nigel was right that blaming all this on Randolph was a cop out. If anything happened to Nyx or Billie Grimm, it would be his responsibility.

Removing his tattered blazer, Nyx lovingly wrapped it around his mother's shoulders. Nyx had checked to make sure Billie was breathing and had a pulse. She felt cold, so he attempted to make her as comfortable as possible. He rubbed her arms hoping to create blood flow and, thus, warmth. She had a golf ball sized lump on her head, but she appeared in pretty decent shape considering. Nyx, on the other hand, had seen better days. He was feeling pain with every breath, but he drove the pain out of his mind. He had too much to do.

"Max," Nyx said, "What's going on?"

"We are trying to move closer to the stage," Max replied.

"I don't think we are under the stage," Nyx said. "There's a shaft up at the top of the cave. It looks like it used to be boarded up."

"You think someone removed the boards?" asked Max.

"No, I think we crashed through them," Nyx answered. "I can't see up the shaft at all. I don't think we fell this whole way. I have a slight recollection of sliding. Did you ever see *The Goonies*?"

"What are Goonies?"

"Never mind," Nyx said. "There's some water down here. I have a feeling it heads to the falls. When Mom comes to, we're going to follow it out of here. Is there any sign of Randolph?"

"None," Max said, "but I can't say that I have been closely watching for him either. Things are very hectic up here."

"I bet," Nyx said as his mom started to move. "Mom's waking up. I'll be in touch, Max."

"Good luck," Max said.

"Nyx?" Billie said. "Oh… what happened?"

"You're going to be okay now Mom. Everything is fine."

"What happened?" she insisted.

"There was an explosion," he answered, "and we fell."

"Where are we?" she said, sitting up with a shiver.

"I'm not sure. I think we are in a cave under the Palmer Inn," he said.

"Are you alright?" Billie asked, seeing the mangled glasses and Nyx's blood-stained face.

"Yes," he said, "I'm fine. I had a bloody nose and I think I bit my tongue."

"Thank goodness," she said, hugging Nyx. Her son cringed at the embrace and grunted in pain. Billie pulled back, looking concerned. "What was that?"

"It's nothing, Mom. I hurt my side."

"Let me see," she said.

"Mom."

"Right now, young man," she insisted.

With some effort, Nyx unbuttoned his dress shirt and opened it. He revealed a huge purple and blue bruise that covered most of Nyx's right side.

"Oh my," Billie said, touching Nyx's injury. He grimaced in pain at her soft touch. "Nyx, you may have broken some ribs."

"I'm fine, Mom," he reassured her with little success.

"No, you are not," Billie said, standing up. "Now, we need to get you to a doctor, right now."

"How do we get out of here?" Nyx said, knowing that there was no use in arguing with her when she got like that, the protective mother bear and her cub. Plus, Nyx *knew* that he required medical attention, but he had hoped this thing with Mr. Randolph would be finished tonight.

"I'm not sure... **arrrggh**," Billie screamed, clutching at her midsection.

"Mom?" said Nyx.

Billie doubled over in pain after the second cramp, and she knelt on the ground.

You've got to be kidding me, Nyx thought.

Chapter Seventeen

Pointing the Way

"I'd like to use a lifeline, Regis."

-Who Wants To Be a Millionaire?

Grasping his mother's hand, Nyx knelt beside her. Billie tried to keep her breathing steady. The last half hour couldn't have been good for his unborn brother or sister, and Nyx cursed himself for not thinking about those possibilities before.

Billie screamed again. This was real, and they were in trouble.

"Mom," Nyx saidas her grip tightened on his hand, "what can I do?"

Reaching into his pocket, Nyx pulled out his phone and tried to dial his father. Nyx was sure that his dad would know what to do, but the technology failed him. There was no signal in this cavern.

"You've got to..." Billie said, closing her eyes and clenching her lips to manage the pain, "get help. Something is wrong. I need you... to ... get help."

"But I don't know where we are. Where do I go?" Nyx said, panicked.

"You can do it, sweetheart," Billie calmly said, "You have to..."

"I don't want to leave you alone, Mom," Nyx said.

"We don't have a choice. I need to get out of here, but I can't go myself. Please..."

Nyx was more scared now than he ever remembered. The only things going through his head was the ways that this could go wrong: he could get lost, he could walk in circles, he could find his way out, but not find his way back, his injuries could prevent him from getting out.

Still, she was right. They could not sit and wait for someone to find them. The risk of waiting outweighed any of the concerns Nyx had.

"Okay, Mom," Nyx said, "I'll go."

He handed her the phone in case the bars would come back, and Nyx kissed his mother on the cheek. Nyx would try to put those negatives out of his mind. There was only one outcome that was acceptable. That outcome was the safety of his mother and unborn sibling, and he would not allow anything else to happen.

"Be careful, son," she said.

Nyx moved away from Billie.

"Max," Nyx whispered, "Mom is in trouble. Something is wrong with the baby. Get an ambulance here as soon as you can, I'm trying to find out where we are."

"It's already on the way," Max said.

The cave traveled in either direction, and Nyx was completely turned around. He hypothesized that the creek within would be flowing toward Lynch Falls, but that was just an educated guess. In fact, it was conceivable that the water could escape the cave in a way that Nyx and his mother couldn't. Images of underground pools with underwater exits flooded Nyx's mind.

A flicker of silvery light from the opposite direction that the water flowed caught Nyx's attention. Something inside him, an intuition of some kind, told him to go that way. So with a final fleeting glimpse back to his mother, Nyx followed the flash into the heart of the cave.

"Max, do you have access to a computer?" Nyx said.

"Yes, I do," he replied.

"Good. See if you can find any old maps of this area, specifically the caves around here. Maybe Nigel could hack into old surveyor records," Nyx said.

"We're on it," Max said.

As Nyx followed the path, he turned a corner only to find the trail fractured into two possible tunnels, one to his left and one to his right.

"Now what?" Nyx said, frustrated. The wrong choice could be catastrophic for his family. He didn't want to leave this monumental decision up to chance like he was Two-Face flipping his scarred two-headed coin.

Just as Nyx was about to choose, a second silver flash in the tunnel to his left sparked. A figure stood inside the darkness of the tunnel, still and apathetic.

"Hello," Nyx called out, excited. "I need help."

The figure did not move as an air of the fantastic possessed the worried teen.

"Hello?" Nyx said again, starting to move into the tunnel toward the mysterious figure. An unnatural chill embraced him with each step as he realized that this wasn't commonplace.

The closer to the figure Nyx got, the more details he could determine. It was a female's build, surrounded by the dull silvery light Nyx had seen before.

"Laura?" Nyx said, taking a guess. "Are you Laura Truman?"

The phantom finally moved her head so Nyx could see her sad face. The spectral form matched the photos of the murdered girl from so many years ago that Nyx had seen during his research of the Palmer Inn. The same murdered girl who was said to haunt the hotel. These paranormal episodes were becoming customary for Nyx.

"Can you help me?" Nyx asked. "My mother's…"

Before Nyx could finish, the phantasm waved her arm to him indicating for Nyx to follow her. The spirit floated gracefully down the passage like a feather falling to the ground. Nyx trailed behind wondering how this weirdness had become his life.

Laura Truman's ghost came to a crevice in the cave wall, and she bolted into it. With an ethereal explosion, the phantom disintegrated in a blinding flash of light. When his eyes cleared, Nyx saw a room past the opening.

Moving quickly inside, there were tons of items: dolls, books, art work. Everything appeared to be undisturbed for years. *A secret room*, Nyx thought. *Laura Truman's secret room.*

In a less time sensitive situation, Nyx would have loved to stop and search through this place for any clues to the cold case, but now was not the time. His mother was waiting for him to help her. In the back of the room, there were a flight of stairs.

"Max, I found some stairs," Nyx said.

"Where do they go?" he replied.

"They go up," Nyx said, feeling like Dr. Peter Venkman.

"Yes, I understand that," said Max, completely missing the *Ghostbusters* allusion. "I meant *where* do they come out at?"

"Never mind, Max," said Nyx, thinking that, if they intended to continue working together, he had to educate Max on some of the finer points of pop culture. "I'm taking them right now."

"Be careful," Max said. "By the way, the ambulance has arrived and so has your father."

"Good," Nyx said.

Taking two steps at a time, Nyx held his right arm tightly against his side. In reality, it didn't help much, but Nyx told himself that it did, and he left it at that. It was a true exhibition of mind over matter at its fullest extreme.

As the stairs came to an end, Nyx found himself facing a solid brick wall.

"I really am in a Scooby Doo Mystery," Nyx said, immediately starting to look for a secret switch of some kind. "It's here… it's got to be here."

Determined, Nyx pushed on the wall and each individual brick. Nyx was not surprised when one of the bricks depressed in and the wall began to slide to the right.

"Jinkies! I knew it!" Nyx said, feeling Velma's catch phrase was called for. Nyx let the sliding wall halt, and he rushed past it.

The sliding brick wall gave way to a small storage room with several tables, chairs, and stools stacked to the ceiling. The surrounding clutter gave the room a claustrophobic feel as Nyx grabbed a chair to jam into the wall's sliding mechanism. Thinking ahead, Nyx did not want to waste time searching for a hidden trigger on a return trip.

Once out of the small room, Nyx found himself in what was clearly, at one time, a tavern. The oval shaped oak bar was at the center of the room with timbered booths, each with detailed designs carved into the wood. The specific story revealed in the designs gave each booth a personality of its own and created a genuine antique piece of artwork that Chumlee from *Pawn Stars* would surely flip over.

Again intrigued, Nyx, nonetheless, continued on his trek. Nyx told himself that when this was all over, he had to come back here for a day of exploring and discovery. But now all he could picture was his mom, prone and in pain, on that cave floor.

Since entering the bar, Nyx could hear voices bleeding through the walls telling him that his destination was close at hand. He could see two exits from the tavern, but one was a better option than the other. Familiar red silk curtains attracted him like a bull to the matador's cape.

Brushing them aside, Nyx found himself back on the dance floor but opposite where he started. Taking a second to breathe as deeply as he could, painfully inhaling precious life supporting oxygen.

"Hey, over here!" Nyx yelled.

"Nyx!" Westley exclaimed, seeing his missing brother. Leaping through the piles of debris, Westley had one thing in mind. He didn't care if it was weird. A second later, he was hugging Nyx as hard as he could.

"Aaaahhhh," Nyx cried from the pain of the hug. "Good to see you too, Westley."

Nyx hastily got free of the embrace. The pain was going to be too much, and he couldn't pass out. Not now.

"Where's Dad?" Nyx asked.

"Nyx!" Richard screamed, answering Nyx's question without Westley's help. Richard started running towards his oldest son. Nyx didn't want another hug of pain, so he knew that he had to think of something real quickly.

"Dad, come on, we've got to get to Mom," Nyx said, moving back toward the bar. "Where are the paramedics?"

Richard stopped in his tracks and yelled, "Hey, get over here now!"

A pair of men came rushing behind Richard pulling a gurney filled with medical supplies and equipment.

"Stay with Max," said Richard to Westley as he followed Nyx into the bar. "Are you alright, son?"

"I'm okay, Dad," Nyx replied. He had no intention of telling his father that he was injured. The broken ribs, if that's what it was, could wait. Billie could not. Nyx led his father and the paramedics into the small storage room where the sliding brick wall remained lodged open.

"Whoa," Richard said as they entered the darkened passageway. "How did you find this, Nyx?"

"I got lucky," he replied, knowing that the answer *I followed Laura Truman's ghost* sounded demented. "This wasn't the only thing I saw down here. It looked like some girl's hidden room."

Reaching the secret room, Richard took a moment to glance around before helping the paramedics carry the gurney.

"I think this stuff used to belong to Laura Truman," Nyx said, as he led them out through the crevice into the main cave.

"How do you know about Laura Truman?" Richard asked.

"Doesn't everyone know about her?" Nyx said.

"I would guess that this place used to be a speakeasy. I bet they brewed alcohol down here during the Prohibition and ran it up to the bar above."

Getting on his radio, Richard called in to the police station the discovery of the enigmatic room. Though Nyx had wanted to go through her things himself, he knew this was the right thing to do. Who knew what the contents of the room might tell experienced investigators?

"Mom is this way," said Nyx.

With the secret room and tunnel behind them, Nyx ran as fast as he could toward the spot where he had left his mother. Richard wondered how Nyx had been so lucky in finding this path, but there would be more chances later to hear his story.

"Mom, I'm back!" Nyx yelled.

No answer came.

"Mom!" Nyx yelled again, seeing Billie motionless on the ground.

Richard sprinted up past Nyx, who had frozen in his tracks. The pulsating despair gushed at the core of Nyx's personage as he watched his father kneel beside his mother. The paramedics scrambled to the woman and immediately got to work. Nyx was struck by the unspoken confidence displayed by his father. There was no inkling of fear on Richard Grimm. He wouldn't allow it. Nyx admired that and wished he could aspire to be like his father.

But the doubt in his soul was threatening to conquer his spirit. Nyx had pushed himself to the brink of his physical capacity to bring help for his mother. The thought of being too late was tormenting his psyche.

The paramedics carefully lifted the woman onto the gurney they had cleared, and then music vital to his wellness guided Nyx to a feeling of euphoria.

"I love you, Richard."

Billie spoke. She was conscious and ostensibly calm. Her voice did not warrant the fear-riddled thoughts surging across her son's subconscious. The continued tranquil conversation between his parents eased the raging apprehension in Nyx's heart.

"Let's get her out of here, boys," Richard said. "Easy does it now."

Richard espied his son still frozen in the exact spot he was when they arrived, and Richard sensed the burden Nyx had on his shoulders. It was a lot for a young teen. Richard approached him with an assured manner.

"She's going to be fine, Nyx," he said, with a strong hand placed gently behind the boy's head.

"What about the baby?" Nyx said.

"That's why we need to get her to the hospital. It looks as if your mother is in labor," Richard said.

"It's... too early," Nyx said.

"It's early, yes, but it's not too early. You were born premature, and I couldn't ask for a stronger, braver son. If the baby takes after you, then he or she will be fine."

The slight blush at the compliment from his father embarrassed Nyx a little. The redness of his cheeks seemed out of place.

"I need you to do one more thing for me, son. I know this is a lot to ask, but I know you can handle it. I need to accompany your mother to the hospital, and we can't delay getting there, so I want you to round up the twins…"

"Max is here," Nyx said, "and he can take us to the hospital with him."

"That's just what I was thinking," Richard said. "I am so proud of you, son."

With those words, Richard hurried to catch up with the paramedics. Nyx stood looking at the pieces of broken wood scattered about the cave floor. A concise glance toward the shaft that he and his mother had slid down affirmed what Nyx already knew. They were lucky. This should have killed them, and the only reason they survived was that they were on the fringe of the stage. Had they been standing where the twins had been standing, there would have been no survival. That explosion was intended to kill Nigel and Westley, no way around it.

According to Julian, Anthony Randolph wanted to control Nyx by breaking him down. Julian may not have been the most reliable witness, but the circumstantial evidence seemed to support him. And Nyx found it hard to believe that Julian would want the twins dead. Julian had plenty of faults but homicidal tendencies were not one of them. At least, that's what Nyx believed.

And Max's stories of Anthony Randolph supported the tales. A man who would murder how many innocent children just to keep himself alive certainly would not think twice about blowing up two teenage boys. This time was close, too close. If Nyx had been a few seconds slower, Westley and Nigel would have paid with their lives for this psycho's obsession. His mother and unborn sibling could have paid the price as well.

Nyx had decided. He was injured, probably with broken ribs, and the night had been an emotional fiasco, but Nyx could not take the chance of a next time. Anthony Randolph had targeted his family in his efforts to get to him, and that was unacceptable. This had to stop, and tonight was the night.

"Max, I need you to round up the twins and get them to a safe location," Nyx said.

"I be fearin' Max cannae do that, Nyx."

"Randolph!"

The Scottish voice bouncing around Nyx's cranium across the com was unmistakable.

"Aye," Randolph said. "I must say to ye boy, ye be impressive. Ye cannae tell from t'packagin', but ye be a fine specimen, lad."

"Where's Max!" Nyx demanded.

"Ah, the comic book connoisseur be fine for now as be yer siblings. But for how long… that be the question."

"What do you want, Randolph?" Nyx exclaimed.

"Ah guess ye'd better be figurin' that out, Nyx," Randolph said just before the disorienting sound of metal being pulverized filled his head. The immutable scratchy buzz that replaced it hummed within his skull. Removing the com unit silenced the hum, but it did not ease the sensation of isolationism, nor did catapulting the com into the nearest cave wall. That did not stop Nyx.

The pain in his side was not helped by his outburst, nor by the violent physical jerk the throwing motion caused. Nyx gulped fast, short breaths trying to maintain his composure, not to mention, his consciousness.

The burst of anger was fleeting. It was now past. It had to be. Nyx could not approach this full of anger. That would make him vulnerable, and that is what Anthony Randolph wanted. Randolph has underestimated Nyx all night, but Nyx could not depend on that again. Randolph had said it himself. He called Nyx a "fine specimen" so flying under the radar looked to be out. Nyx was the Conduit, and that made him special. He told himself that fact over and again. Seeing what he had accomplished so far tonight, he even started to fool himself into believing.

"Okay Mr. Randolph," a defiant Nyx said, "you want me, you got me."

Retracing the path, Nyx began the climb up the hidden stairs to face his destiny.

Chapter Eighteen

Psybolt Out of the Blue

"There can be only one."

-Connor MacLeod
Highlander

The Palmer Inn

The sliding brick wall

Saturday, 7:12 PM

Standing beside the still jammed secret brick wall, Nyx paused to think about the evening's incidents at the most eventful dance Nyx had ever attended. The Sadie Hawkins dance would certainly always be remembered by the populace of Parker's Point High School, though, more than likely, not for positive reasons.

Nyx had crossed through Laura Truman's hidden room on his way out of the cavern below Palmer Inn. There were already uniformed police officers treating the hidden room like a crime scene. They were bagging everything into evidence and hauling objects away. Nyx thought about asking for help, but he stopped short. There were too many questions that Nyx could not answer for them. Questionsthat could not be answered by Nyx without delving into the secret of the Conduit such as why was the school's guidance counselor chasing him or why would the school's guidance counselor want to hurt the twins in the first place. Plus, there was something inside Nyx that wanted to be the one to end this madness. Randolph had targeted Nyx's family, and Nyx was ready to finish this, to protect his family once and for all.

Nyx exited the back room and crossed through the bar to the last place he had seen the twins. The dance floor was mostly deserted now, though a few police officers remained to close off the stage.

Ye begettin' warmer, Nyx, lad.

The voice in his head truly disturbed Nyx as he had already gotten rid of the com unit Max had given him. So it was true. Anthony Randolph was a mentalist. They had been hemming around that all night. Julian had indicated that Randolph had mind control abilities, and now it looked like telepathy was one of the skills as well.

I'm coming, Psybolt, Nyx thought. He didn't know if Randolph heard him, but it didn't matter. Nyx knew he would find him, and that this mess would end tonight.

Nyx was so focused on the voice invading his head that he lost track of his personal vicinity. His surroundings blended into the background noise of his life. Even an exclamation of his own name did not snap him from his trance. So the pain from the impromptu hug shocked the geek back into reality.

"Ow," Nyx said, as Helena clenched him tightly.

"I can't believe that you're alive," Helena said, not noticing that her embrace was causing Nyx pain. He squirmed free, grasping his side in anguish. "Oh, I'm sorry. Are you alright?"

"Yeah, I'm… fine," Nyx coughed out. The flash of whiteness across his face told a different story.

"You're hurt," Helena said, gently placing her arm on his shoulder. "You need to see a doctor."

Helena's concern was sweet, but Nyx wasn't going anywhere.

"No, I'm fine," he said.

"No, you are not," said Julian, walking over to the pair. "Helena's right. You're hurt, and you need to go to the hospital."

"I have something to do first," said Nyx. "I'll go after that."

Nyx and Julian made eye contact. The determination of the young geek reeked off him like a stench, a sight that Julian had seen before.

"You're going after Randolph, aren't you?" Julian said.

"Wait," Helena said, "what?"

"That's it, isn't it? You're going after Randolph. Don't be a fool. In your condition, you wouldn't stand a chance."

"Why would Nyx be going after Mr. Randolph?" Helena asked.

"I have no choice," Nyx said.

"You always have a choice," Julian said. "Let's get you home."

"He has Westley and Nigel," Nyx said, stopping Julian in his tracks. "And Max, too. Maybe he picked up that trick from someone."

Julian turned his head from the less than subtle slam from his former best friend.

"Wait… are you saying Mr. Randolph kidnapped your brothers?" Helena questioned.

"I didn't want any of this to happen, Nyx. I'm sorry it has," said Julian.

"Sorry doesn't really do much for me right now," said Nyx.

"Nyx, there are police officers here," Helena said, "If Mr. Randolph has kidnapped Westley and Nigel, then we should get the police to help us."

Helena started to move toward the police near the stage, but Nyx reached out and snagged her arm. The effort of his grab sent shockwaves of agony through his body. Gritting his teeth, Nyx forced the pain down once again.

"No… the police can't help. Just trust me Helena… I've got to do this myself," Nyx said.

"No, you don't," Julian said. "I can help you."

"No," Nyx said.

"I know Randolph," Julian said. "I know his weaknesses and his plans. I can help you stop him and save Westley and Nigel."

"No," said Nyx again.

"Why not?" Julian asked.

"Because I don't trust you. For all I know, this is still part of your plan to get even with me," Nyx said as Julian looked like a whipped puppy.

"I'm sorry," Julian said.

"I don't understand any of this," Helena said.

"If you truly want to help me, Julian, take Helena home. Get her out of here, and get her to a place where she'll be safe. That way there will be one less person I have to worry about," Nyx said.

Still reeling from Nyx's words, Julian dejectedly nodded.

"No, I'm not going anywhere," Helena said, crossing her arms in front of her, "not if you are staying. If you stay, so do I."

"Helena," said Nyx, looking into her face, "you need to go with Julian. I can't explain why, but you've got to believe me, I can't be worried about you too. My brothers are missing, my mother is in labor, and Max could be in mortal danger. Please don't be another person in my life that I have to be scared for."

Helena dropped the attitude, and gently swaddled her arms around Nyx's neck.

"Be careful," she whispered in his ear, acquiescing to his wishes.

Breaking away, Nyx held Helena's arm.

"I'll be fine," he said. He didn't convince either of them. As he started to leave, Nyx turned back to Julian. "You know, you were right."

"About what?" he asked.

"Psybolt *does* make a better villain than hero," Nyx said.

With that reference back to happier times playing *Capes and Cowls* with Julian and their role-playing group in the back room at Bright's Comix, Nyx turned away again heading nowhere in particular, but right for the danger that awaited him. Julian and Helena watched as a hero small of stature but large of heart headed up the stairs.

Nyx always knew where this was going to end up. He had known since yesterday when his mom and siblings visited Palmer Inn. He didn't verbalize it, but the juxtaposition between present and past was too obvious to be ignored. And now with Max involved, it was a certainty that Randolph couldn't avoid the poetry of the situation.

Opening the glass doors, Nyx walked outside onto the overhang above Lynch Falls. Anthony Randolph, looking weak, leaned against the railing, smiling his evil smile at Nyx.

"I knew ye would find yer way here," said Randolph.

Nyx looked around, slowly stepping out to the wooden deck. Westley and Nigel stood petrified on each side of the overhang with blank expressions, the cool wind softly blowing their ragged sandy hair. The absence of anything that made the twins the twins was extremely disturbing. Nyx wanted to hear them arguing about something stupid… who's stronger: Superman or the Hulk? Who's better in a fight: Captain America or Batman? But there would be no argument made. Silence was not golden.

"This is over," Nyx said.

"Aye, ah agree, lad," said Randolph.

"Where's Max?" Nyx asked.

Randolph smiled. "Irony be a wonderful thin,' aye?"

With a gesture of his right thumb, Randolph pointed over his shoulder toward the waterfall. Nyx leaned over the side to look. Tied and gagged, Max hung from the deck directly behind Randolph.

"Why is there always someone tied up and dangling?" Nyx said.

"Ah thought ye might appreciate that," said Randolph, "but when yer brother was tied, a fall wouldn't be as fatal, aye?"

"You're crazy, Randolph," said Nyx. "There are police all over the place here. There's no way you can get away with this."

"Ha ha ha," laughed Randolph. "Are ye bloody serious? Ah can do whatever ah be wantin.' The police mean nothin' to me. They ain't never goin' ta see us. Ah made sure o' that."

"You've been manipulating everything lately, haven't you, Anthony? Like when you murdered Rex Riley to make sure that the dance would be held here."

"Murdered? Dinnae ye hear? Rex Riley committed suicide," Randolph laughed.

"Helped along by you right?" said Nyx.

"And?"

"What kind of monster are you? He was your childhood friend, and you treat him like a piece of garbage."

"Ye condemn me fer that? Rex Riley was as evil o' a human being t' ever cross yer path. Who knows how many lives were saved by his death? Ah should be given a medal," said Randolph.

"What about those children in Scotland? Do you want a medal for them as well?" Nyx sarcastically said.

"Ah did what had to be done to survive," Randolph said. "Anyone would have done the same thing."

"No they wouldn't," said Nyx.

"Do not talk like ye understand, boy. When was the last time ye suffered from an inoperable brain tumor… a brain tumor that was killing ye slowly and painfully? Until ya go through what ah went through, you be havin' no right to say anythin' ta me."

"Is that what you told Diego when you killed him?"

Randolph was taken aback by the words of the young geek. He subconsciously reached for the scars on temples.

"So ye been doin' yer homework, I see," Randolph said.

"He saved you from your tumor, and then you killed him," Nyx said, really guessing more than anything. He knew some basic details that Max had provided, but most of it was speculation.

"Aye, that he did. He did more than save me… because o' him, ah be reborn. His process o' removin' the tumor had a side effect that no one be expectin'. Triggered something inside me mind. Me dear master Diego made me what I be today," Randolph said.

"And you killed him," Nyx said.

"He outlived his usefulness. The accident robbed him of his mind… he dinnae want to live as a vegetable for the rest o' his life. Ah did him a favor," Randolph said. "He saved me, ah saved him."

"Now that your brain tumor is back, I bet you wish he was here," Nyx said.

"What? Are ye daft, Nyx? Me tumor be not back," Randolph said.

"Of course it is," said Nyx, suddenly not as confident as he had felt. "That's why you want me. That's why you're looking like death warmed over."

"Aha ha ha," laughed Randolph. "Wrong, but a good guess. Ah would say that ye be close."

"Then why are you doing all of this if you are not dying again?" Nyx asked.

"When ah awoke from me swim with Max, ah had washed up on the Scottish shore, but ah may as well have died at sea. Ah knew ah had a short time remainin'. And then me luck changed. Diego found me and saved me with his psychic surgery. Ah awoke from that procedure different, powerful, dominant."

Randolph turned slightly to look out over the waterfall.

"Me own power surpassed that of Diego. I had absolute power," Randolph said. "There's always a price for absolute power."

"A price?" Nyx said.

"Aye, a price. A side effect of me gainin' these mental powers... the more ah used 'em, the weaker ah grew."

"Like an endurance drain," said Nyx, understanding the concept from comics.

"Aye, somethin' like that, but it be worse. Ah found, the more ah used me abilities, the more ah slipped into madness," said Randolph.

Nyx had him talking, but he wasn't sure what he could do. In fact, it was possible that Randolph would know what he was going to do before Nyx even did it. Nyx struggled to keep his mind blank while the villain rattled on with his story. Clearly, Anthony Randolph wanted to tell someone of his plight.

"Diego saved me again," he continued. "Ah was able to drain some of his mental energy from him and that sustained me. It made me whole again."

"So you're a parasite... living off another living thing," Nyx said.

"Aye, in a sense, that be true."

"You're a tapeworm," Nyx said.

"Now, dinnae be cruel. This relationship worked for us for several years, until just over a year ago when Diego was in his accident and rendered helpless," said Randolph.

A biting shudder staggered the eldest Grimm child as he didn't need to be Sherlock Holmes to deduce where this tale was heading. He didn't just want to control him, as Julian had said, but he wanted a symbiotic relationship. He wanted to feed off him.

"You needed a replacement for Diego..." Nyx started.

"An' who better than the bloody Conduit? A boy who be consistently in contact with the Prophesight, the psychic energy o' the entire world. Aye, that be perfect."

"Like an all you can eat buffet," Nyx snapped.

"Aye," Randolph said, "That be funny, lad."

"So why target Westley and Nigel?" Nyx asked.

"Ah knew Bright was here, and that ye wouldn't be anxious to join me," Randolph said.

"Ya think?" Nyx said.

"So ah decided that ye be needin' ta be broken down. It was obvious that the twins meant a lot to ye… much as me own brothers meant to me. That be the worst day in me life. Fletcher and Wallace died before me eyes. Ah saw the bomb that took their lives. An' there be nothin' ah could do. Ah knew how long it took for me ta recover… by then, ye would be mine."

"That's really sick," said Nyx, "and cruel. Nigel and Westley never did anything to you, and yet you were willing to sacrifice them just to get what you wanted."

"Aye, that be so," Randolph agreed.

"And yet *I* saved *my* brothers when you *couldn't* save *yours*," Nyx taunted. "So what now?"

Randolph dropped the smile that he had been sporting since Nyx walked out on the overhang. The dig at his pain was unexpectedly dirty. There was no pity from Nyx for the terrible life Anthony Randolph had lived. There was no understanding for the horrific choices that he had to make. This teenage brat stood defiantly before him, flaunting his power that could give Anthony immortality.

"What now?" snapped Randolph. "Maybe ye do need to feel a little tragedy in yer life, punk."

Without a movement, even as much as a blink, the telepathic message emerged inside the controlled minds of the twins. Westley and Nigel each climbed up on the railing above the power of Lynch Falls. They balanced precariously atop the thin beam, one step leading to tragedy.

"So Mr. Hero," Randolph said, "ye may reach one o' the young Brothers Geek if'n yer lucky, but there be no way to reach them both. Tell me Nyx Grimm, what do ye do?"

"Leave them alone!" Nyx said. "I'll go with you. You can do whatever you have to as long as you let them alone."

"Nae, ah do not believe ye. Yer spirit be too strong, and that be leadin' to yer attempt to escape from me clutches. An' ah cannae be havin' that."

"No, I promise, I swear… just leave them alone," Nyx screamed.

"Ye never know, lad. The twins be young. They may survive the drop. I did, five years ago," Randolph said, looking at the entangled Max Bright. "Ain't that right, Maxie ol' boy?"

"Please," Nyx pleaded.

"Och, ah'm tired o' waitin' fer ye to decide. Say goodbye boys," Randolph said.

But before the lethal mental order could be executed, deafening electronic notes blared from the opened glass doors, decibels shaking the windows. The words from Nerf Herder boomed across the deck.

The whispers in the hall never bother her at all,
Or the laughter from the boys in the gymnasium,
Frauline Mueller is alarmed at the scratches on her arm,
And the German homework is late again, oh no,
She's a Sleestak
She's a Sleestak
She's a Sleestak
She's a Sleestak

Julian leaned against the giant speakers that the DJ had been using for the dance, as the woofers rattled with each sound. Randolph covered his ears, squinted his eyes, and withdrew from the piercing tune.

"Oswald, what be ye doin', ye traitor?" Randolph exclaimed.

"This one goes to eleven," Julian yelled, barely audible over the music.

When the music started to bellow, the twins revived as if waking from a dream.

"What the…" Nigel, who had been facing the waterfall, stumbled back from his perch and landed hard on the wooden deck. Westley's awakening was a little more graceful as he hopped down from the top of the rail.

His brothers safe, and the song's frenetic cadence still pounding away, Nyx moved on Anthony Randolph. The counselor maintained his recession from the music, ears covered as tightly as he could.

"Come on, Anthony, that song is not that bad," Nyx said, grabbing Randolph by his white coat collar and slamming his back into the rail. Nyx was feeling no pain, as his body jazzed up like he had taken an Underdog super energy pill. Nyx was not sure what to do next, not even remotely being an expert in fighting. Nyx buried a right jab into Randolph's ribs, wanting him to feel the pain that he had felt. Nyx realized right away that the punch left a great deal to be desired. Strength was not Nyx's strength.

Randolph, already physically debilitated from the over use of his mental powers, weakly tried to fight back. Randolph brought an elbow into Nyx's injured side as if he knew exactly where the damage had been done. The surgical strike broke the grip of his attacker as Nyx stumbled back a step, grasping at the pain in hisside.

With the moment's respite, Randolph reached over the rail for Max, his final card up his sleeve.

"No!" yelled Nyx, rushing at Randolph before the mentalist could do whatever he was planning. The young boy smashed into Randolph with such force that both of them were propelled past the rail and tumbled over the side. A scream faded into the evening sky as the final chords of the Nerf Herder song culminated.

"Nyx!" screamed Nigel.

"Please God, no!" Westley said, dashing over to the rail where the two rivals had disappeared into the darkness of the night.

Westley compelled himself to look over the side. Forcing his eyes open as Nigel hurried to join by his side, Westley prepared himself for the mournful fate suffered by his brother.

"Nyx!" Westley hollered, seeing his brother's left arm desperately hooked to the bondage that had secured Max. Max had part of his arm free and had a death grip on Nyx's shirt. Nyx's legs kicked against the pull of gravity that struggled, begged, for a second victim. There was no sign of Anthony Randolph amidst the waves of mist peppering from the waterfall.

"Pull us up!" Nyx yelled, straining every muscle in his arm to prevent his own fall.

With Julian and the twins helping, they were able to first pull Nyx and then Max back up on the deck. As Westley and Julian began to work on untying Max, Nigel placed his arm around Nyx's shoulders.

"Nice job, Buffy," he said.

"Thanks, Xander," Nyx replied.

Finally free of the bondage, Max struggled to his feet and dragged himself over to Nyx.

"Thank you, my boy. I was worried for a minute that you were going to wind up like Sherlock Holmes and Professor Moriarty, falling to their death in Conan Doyle's *The Final Problem*."

Nyx looked at Max.

"You're not the only one who can use pop culture references," Max said proudly.

"We'll have to work on that," said Nyx.

"Yeah, pop culture means something from this century," Nigel said, "...or maybe the previous one."

"Nice try, though," said Westley.

Chapter Nineteen

Friends and Family

"We're the good guys, Michael"

Benjamin Linus
LOST
"Live Together, Die Alone"

The three Grimm boys sat together in the waiting room at the Parker's Point hospital awaiting news. Max had brought them to the hospital last night after finally getting away from the Palmer Inn. Nyx, Westley and Nigel did not get much sleep in the uncomfortable chairs. Several times the nurses would come in and offer to take them to separate rooms where they might get more rest, but they refused. After the night they had, they just wanted to stay together, and the worry over their mother kept them spurred on.

Ariel had been staying at her babysitter since last night. The babysitter was pressed into extra duty with the results of the evening's events. Richard, who was supposed to pick Ariel up when he got off work, had come directly to the hospital with Billie and had only come out a couple of times during the night to check on the boys. It had been three hours since Richard had made an appearance, though and the boys had become concerned.

Max had stayed in the hospital with them, but he was out of sight. He had had a rough evening as well. It's not too often that someone is dangled off a deck above a waterfall. Max could honestly say that was the first time that had happened to him.

When the twins had questioned Nyx last night about Anthony Randolph's fate, Nyx was not sure what to say.

"I don't know what happened," Nyx had said. "As we went over the side, I was able to snag Max's ropes and I held on for all I could. I didn't want to look down."

"I did," Max continued. "I saw him fall. I watched him disappear into the mist below, and I know this is not the Christian way, but I hope he suffered before he died."

The wind softly blew the smell of the trees through the air, and Nyx looked out over the continuous falling of the water. The weight of the evening had burdened Nyx.

"What is it, Nyx?" Max asked.

Nyx paused before he said, "Did I do the right thing? I may have…
killed him."

Max said, "Of course, Nyx, you saved my life. How can you doubt
yourself? You did what you had to do."

"Yeah, sometimes you do what you have to," said Nigel.

"Right, I mean," Westley said, "Han shot first. He knew he was
protecting himself and his crew. That's all you were doing."

"Han didn't shoot first in the special edition. Greedo shot first in that
film," said Nigel.

"Blasphemy!" shouted Westley.

The sound of the twins arguing once again was music to Nyx's ears
and went further to ease his nagging uneasiness than anything.

As of this morning, the police had yet to recover Anthony Randolph's
body, and Nyx was careful about believing it was over. Randolph had
survived a fall like this before, who's to say that he couldn't have done it
again?

Before bringing the boys to the hospital, Max carefully made sure
that evidence was found that implicated Randolph in the bombing at the
dance. Nyx was a little uncertain if they should be planting evidence, but
he knew that Randolph was guilty, so he saw no harm. It was not as if they
were making the evidence up, they were just making sure that the police
were able to find it.

With heavy eyelids, Nyx leaned back in the chair, hoping to catch
himself a few winks of sleep, but a random glance at the muted television
playing brought him back to full diligence. On the screen there was a
photo of Laura Truman.

"Hey," Nyx said, scurrying to the television to turn it up, "look
there."

"… over twenty year old case appears to be solved. Police this morning
arrested retired lawyer David Wise. Though police would not comment
on the case, officials stated that recent evidence pointed to Wise, and that
the case was, quote, strong."

As the newscast changed stories, Nyx muted the television once again
returning to his seat.

"What was that about?" asked Westley.

"It's nothing," Nyx said, "just one less cold case."

"Nyx… Nyx… wake up."

Richard stood over his slumbering son who had finally dozed off. He really didn't want to disturb him. He knew he had had a tough twenty four hours, but he also knew the news he had to give would be a relief. Westley and Nigel were rolled up in nearby chairs snoring loudly. Westley's temporary cast was placed tenderly beneath his head. Richard decided to let the twins sleep, but he had to tell someone.

"Nyx… wake up, son."

The flittering lashes attempted to clear the blurriness from his sight as the boy wiped the sleep from the corners of his eyes. A deep yawn slipped from his throat forcing those same eyes to water ever so slightly. The replacement of his glasses cleared the picture of the world around him.

"Dad?" Nyx muttered as the clouds brightened, and he began to understand where he was. The twenty five minute nap made Nyx feel worse than if he hadn't slept at all. "What is it?"

"Son, you have a new brother," Richard said.

"Mom?"

"She's fine. It was a difficult labor, but she pulled through like a trooper," said Richard.

"And the baby?"

"The baby is fine, healthy. You'll have to come and see him later this afternoon. How are you feeling, Nyx?"

Nyx had been x-rayed when he arrived at the hospital, and they revealed that he had broken three ribs, the 7th, 8th, and 10th ones. The doctors prescribed simple ibuprofen as a manner of managing the pain. They told him that the ribs would heal on their own.

"I'm sore," Nyx answered, "but I think I am okay."

"Good," said Richard. "When your brothers wake up, you'll let them know about their baby brother, right?"

"Yes," Nyx said.

"Would you keep an eye on your brothers while I go pick up Ariel?"

"Yes," Nyx said.

As his father departed the waiting room, Nyx rolled his neck from side to side letting one more yawn slip free. There would be no more chances for sleep now. He was saddled with his brothers once again. Nyx was alright with that.

The four Grimm children, reunited, followed their father down the antiseptic filled hallway toward their mother's room. Even Ariel was excited about the new baby. Typical concerns about the youngest being threatened by a new arrival did not appear to be coming to fruition as Ariel had been practically jumping since the news of the premature birth reached her. A baby brother was what she had wanted, and now she had it.

Westley's memories had completely resurfaced, remembering his hand in the defacing of the living room. The young boy's guilt came pouring out when he and his brothers were alone, but they both eased his conscience. Westley had no way of controlling what he had done. The mental suggestions by Anthony Randolph were just too strong. Nyx suggested that they let it be, and they allow the world to believe that Rex Riley indeed was the culprit. Rex had confessed, after all.

None of that seemed important right now, though, as the Grimm family entered the hospital room. Billie Grimm sat in her bed, and her tired smile did not cover the fatigue that had overtaken her.

"My loves," she said.

Unable to contain herself any more, Ariel ran over to the bed and leapt onto it. Billie cradled her sole daughter close to her.

"It is so good to see all of you," she said.

"Where's the baby?" Ariel asked.

"Oh, sweetie, the baby is in the NICU," said Billie.

"What's that?" she asked.

"That's the neonatal intensive care unit," Billie answered.

"Intensive care?" Westley said. "Everything is alright, isn't it?"

"Of course it is, Westley." Richard said.

"With any preemie, there is caution. The baby being born early means that he may not have fully developed organs, and there are precautions that the hospital takes to make sure that he is healthy. Nyx was born premature, and he turned out fine."

"What's his name?" Nigel asked, not able to hold back any further. The name had been a subject of considerable debate amongst the boys since the sex of the baby was revealed. They knew that their mother had won the bet, and that she had earned the right to name. Nyx worried about the result since. Already with the names Nyx, Westley, Nigel and Ariel in tow, it would almost be better for the baby if they just left it as Baby Boy Grimm.

"His name is Napoleon James Grimm," Billie answered.

Napoleon? Nyx thought.

"That's a *DYNAMITE* name, Mom," said Nigel, pleased with the quick-witted pun that he had spit out.

"We can call him Nap," she said.

Parker's Point High School

Hallway

Monday, 8:10 AM

Another week of school started without even a glance behind to the results of the weekend. It was better that way. A Monday represented a new week and a fresh start. The week past filled with suicides, terrorists, bombings, and betrayals by school personnel was put aside and restarted anew.

However, a few of the wounds remained, a few plot points dangled for the Brothers Geek, and it was clear that they would not be able to ignore the past like the rest of the school as Nigel said that Monday morning, "Uber Geek coming."

Julian approached with his head down. Nyx knew this was inevitable.

"Nyx, Westley, Nigel," Julian said, "are you guys alright?"

"We're fine, Julian," Nyx said.

"My mom told me that your mom is doing well," Julian said. "I thought about coming to see you at the hospital yesterday, but I decided it was better to stay away."

"Thanks," Nyx said. The twins were atypically silent. Neither had a smart aleck remark to make nor did they leave. They wanted to hear what Julian had to say.

"I know I've done a lot to you guys," Julian started, "and I am not here to make excuses. I made plenty of mistakes that I regret, and that I wish I could take back. But I can't. I have to live with the choices that I made. For what it's worth, I just want to let you know that I am sorry for my part in this mess."

Julian began to turn away, but Nyx grabbed ahold of his arm.

"Hold on Julian," Nyx said. "I know what you've done, and I would be lying if I said that I could completely forget it."

Julian's head sagged in disappointment.

"But," Nyx continued, "you saved Westley and Nigel's life on that deck Saturday. If you had not stepped in, there would be no way that I could have saved them both. And we all know that Anthony Randolph could make people do things against their will. Though I may not be able to forget what you've done, I can forgive. I think you've earned a second chance from me."

Julian smiled at Nyx who extended his hand to the Uber Geek.

"Thank you for saving the twins' life," Nyx said.

Julian accepted the handshake and said, "You're welcome."

"This feels right," said Westley. "We're complete again."

With that seal of approval from Westley, Julian acknowledged the twins with a slight nod of the head, and he turned to head to his first period class.

"Oh, Nyx, by the way," Julian said, stopping. "I just wanted you to be aware that Helena and I are not together. That relationship was never real."

"Why are you telling me that?" Nyx asked.

"Oh, I don't know," Julian said, cracking a smile. "See you guys later."

After the assembly of the Brothers Geek in the hallway, Nyx was en route to Mrs. Templeton's science class when he was stopped once again by the call of his name.

"Nyx," Helena said, back in her leather outfit she had discarded for the weekend past's functions. "Hold on, Nyx."

"Hi Helena," Nyx said.

"How are you?" she asked.

"I'm okay. My side hurts, but I got good drugs," Nyx joked, hoping to break the tension he was feeling.

"Congratulations," she said with a laugh. Nyx's tension breaking attempt was a true failure. "How's your mother?"

"She's okay," Nyx said. "She had the baby."

"Yeah, I heard that you now have another little brother, huh? I'm so very happy for you," Helena responded.

"Thanks," Nyx said.

Helena said, "Um... Nyx, I just wanted to say..."

"Helena," interrupted Nyx, "you don't have to say anything."

"But I do," she said. "I am sorry. I like you. I like you a lot. I hope what I did isn't going to ruin what could be great."

"I liked you too," Nyx said.

"Liked?" Helena asked.

"Give me some time, Helena. The things that happened are still pretty fresh."

"Yeah," she said. "I get it."

"But, I liked being with you, and it is not something that I want to give up yet," Nyx said, "so, just be patient. I forgave Julian; I think I can forgive you, too."

"Good," she said, a load lifted from her. She took a step closer to Nyx and planted a soft kiss on his cheek. With a wink, Helena turned to leave. Nyx walked inside the science room. An engrossed Helena walked down the hall inattentive of the world around her. She bumped into Mandy.

"Sorry," Helena said to no one in particular.

Mandy's face darkened with defiance as the light died from her. Nyx and Helena had been oblivious to her as she stared at their hallway meeting with strained, doubtful eyes. The tightness of her lips accompanied the gut-wrenching intensity the young freshman girl suddenly felt. Glaring with her green-eyed glare at the departure of the Goth, Mandy felt the fierce tic pulling at the corner of her lip.

"I don't think so," Mandy said.

Staring at the name tag on the crib, Nyx couldn't believe that it actually said ***Napoleon James Grimm***.

"Looks like Mom and Dad struck again," said Nyx. "Sorry, buddy."

The NICU was overwhelming to Nyx when he first stepped into the room. The amount of equipment that little Nap was hooked up to scared Nyx for a second. He had pulled up a web site before entering the room, but it failed to provide him with an ample real life feel that this room did.

Nyx was the first of the children to be allowed to visit Nap. The others would have to wait until the baby was a little stronger and was hooked up to fewer machines. But Nyx had really proven his strength to his parents over the last few days, and they thought some time alone would be a good opportunity for them to bond.

"Hey, I'm Nyx," he said, looking through the clear plastic tent that surrounded the baby. "I'm your big brother. Mom and Dad tell me that I was a preemie as well. I guess I had all this stuff fastened to me as well, so there is no reason to be afraid. You're going to be just fine."

Pulling the wooden rocking chair over to the crib, Nyx sat down, and he began to rock nervously.

"Of course, it would be better if you took after our sister Ariel or our Dad," Nyx said. "Maybe Mom... the rest of us are... well, we're geeks. Okay, Dad is a geek too, but he's a cop so that's kind of mitigating circumstances."

The nurse walked over to the crib, and she checked Nap's instruments. She smiled at Nyx, and she wrote down something on the chart that hung on the crib before exiting the room.

"You have two other brothers, Nigel and Westley. They argue all the time, but they are good guys. Don't tell them that. They're annoying enough as it is," Nyx said. "Boy, you're small, Nap."

His mother had told Nyx that Napoleon would be small. The doctors said he was born with "low birth weight" which was better than some preemies. Nap weighed just over 4 pounds at birth. Nyx, always being small himself, wondered how much being a preemie led to his own personal challenges.

"I have to tell you something," Nyx said, checking the area to make sure that they were out of earshot of anyone else. "It's a secret, so you have to promise me that you won't tell anyone, 'k?"

Nyx waited a second as if he was waiting for an answer.

"Okay, I'm trusting you now," he continued. "See, I am the Conduit. I know you don't know what that is, but that's not important. What you need to know is, because I am the Conduit, strange things may happen to me. There may be times where I am in danger. I just want you to know that I will **never** let that hurt you or touch you. I will do everything that I can to make sure that you are always safe and loved."

Nyx placed his hand on top of the tent.

"Whether you want it or not, you are now officially a Brother Geek."

Epilogue

The Price of Absolute Power

"And I would have gotten away with it too, if it hadn't been for those meddling kids."

-Scooby Doo, Where Are You?

Dr. Ryan Collins studied the charts of the most recently admitted patient. It was a curious case, as the precipitating factors to the breakdown were a mystery. Dr. Collins loved this kind of mystery. It was the reason he became a doctor.

Walking slowly down the hallway, Dr. Collins stopped at the room where the newest arrival was held. A simple exchange with the guard led to the opening of the door.

Entering the padded room, Dr. Collins saw that his patient had crawled into the far corner and had wedged himself in, both feet dug into the floor, arms wrapped around his torso and secured in the back.

"How are we today, Anthony?" Dr. Collins asked.

There was no response from the bald headed man. Dr. Collins was not surprised by that. Since he was brought into the asylum, Anthony had spoken only a few words and those were incoherent ramblings with a Scottish accent.

An incident with a nurse and his medication led to the restraint Anthony found himself trapped in. Each time the doctors attempted to remove the straitjacket, Anthony would do something violent leading him right back into the deterrent.

Dr. Collins moved close to his patient, and he was concerned by the lack of even the merest flicker of the eyelids, a blink. Dr. Collins looked deep into his eyes, searching for recognition of any kind. He only found a great void.

After a quick examination, Dr. Collins knocked on the door as a signal to let him out. This man had only deteriorated since his arrival a few days ago, and there was no reason for such a condition, at least, not one that the doctors could find. There were scars on the man's head, but those were from several years prior. Whatever had happened to him had happened recently.

Walking into the waiting room, the young man who had admitted him stood staring out the window at the tranquil environment surrounding this locale, waiting patiently for word from the doctor. Julian turned to Dr. Collins as he approached him.

"I'm sorry to inform you, but Anthony does not seem to be responding to anything that we have tried so far," said Dr. Collins.

"Oh no," said Julian, "I do hope that you aren't giving up, Dr. Collins. I would hate to believe that Uncle Anthony was a lost case."

"No, we haven't given up. We are going to continue to be as aggressive as we can, but I just want you to understand that it might take quite a while before we see any progress."

"Doctor, I understand completely, and that is fine with me. I have heard that it is better to take things slow. Uncle Anthony used to tell me that all the time," Julian said through a smile with nothing behind it but teeth. The sinister sparkle in the teen's eyes chronicled the baneful musings of vengeance buried beneath the mask of friendship. "A slow burn."

Geek Glossary II: The Sequel

*Once again, there are many terms contained within **Psybolt Unleashed** that, if you are not a geek, you may not recognize. For those out there, here is the second edition of the Geek Glossary to increase your geek vocabulary.*

Arturo, Professor Maximillion: n *Sci-Fi* character from television program called *Sliders*. Professor Arturo was portrayed by John Rhys-Davies from 1995 to 1997. The character of Professor Arturo was shot and supposedly killed in the third season.

Ashburn, Aubrey: n *Music*singer, songwriter originally from Cleveland, Ohio. Ashburn performed the song "I Am the One" from the soundtrack of Dragon Age and won "Best Original Song for a Video Game" at the *Hollywood Music in Media Awards.*

A-Team, The: n *TV* television program that aired from 1983-1987 on NBC that starred George Peppard, Mr. T, Dirk Benedict, and Dwight Schultz. *The A-Team* was made into a feature film in 2010.

Avengers, The: n *Marvel Comics* Super hero team called "Earth's Mightiest Heroes" were created by Stan Lee and Jack Kirby. The Avengers roster has fluctuated over the years, but most consider the main members to include the "big three" of Captain America, Iron Man, and Thor.

Bauer, Jack: n *TV* television character played by Kiefer Sutherland on FOX Network's *24*. Jack Bauer was an agent for the fictional CTU. Jack would race against the clock in attempts to foil the latest terrorist plot, showing amazing resiliency.

Beast, the: n *Marvel Comics* Scientist Hank McCoy is the comic book super hero known as the Beast. Beast was an original member of the X-Men, but became well known when he mutated into a blue, fur covered hero. Beast was also a member of the Avengers.

Black Eyed Peas, the: n *Music* American hip hop group formed in Los Angeles in 1995. Group includes will.i.am, Fergie, apl.de.ap, and Taboo.

Black Ops: n *Video Games Call of Duty: Black Ops* is a first-person shooter video game by Activision that came out in 2010. This video game is, for the first time in the series, set in the Cold War.

Bowen Designs: n *Statues* company that deals with the creation and sale of entertainment- based statues. Bowne Designs has specialized in creating statues of characters from Marvel Comics, but has also branched out to other areas. Randy Bowen is the primary designer and sculptor.

Buffy, the Vampire Slayer: n *TV* television program produced by Joss Whedon that followed the exploits of Buffy Summers, the "chosen" vampire slayer. *Buffy, the Vampire Slayer* ran for five seasons on the WB Network and two more on UPN. Sarah Michelle Gellar starred as Buffy Summers.

Champions: n *Role-Playing Games* RPG produced by Hero Games that focuses on the universal Hero System to create super hero characters. Champions is currently in their 6th edition.

Chumlee: n *TV* one of the stars of the History Channel's reality program, *Pawn Stars*, "Chumlee," whose real name is Austin Russell, works at the Gold & Silver Pawn Shop where the show is filmed.

CTU: n *TV* fictional governmental agency from FOX's television series *24*. The Counter-Terrorism Unit was the backdrop for the series and agent Jack Bauer from the beginning. CTU was based out of Los Angeles for most of the run of the show.

David Letterman pencil trick: n *TV* a trick David Letterman performs on his late night talk show where he flips a pencil into the air and catches it while watching himself on a monitor giving the impression that he was not looking.

Dragon Age: Origins: n *Video Games* a single player role-playing video game by Electronic Arts. The game was released in 2009. Players assume the role of a mage, warrior or rogue in an attempt to unite the kingdom of Ferelden to fight a demonic invasion.

Dungeons & Dragons: n *Role-Playing Games* abbreviated D & D, the game was created by Gary Gygax and Dave Arnston in 1974. D & D's publication was considered the beginning of the RPG industry. D & D is the most successful RPG of all time spawning films, cartoons and books.

Endurance drain: n *Role-Playing Games* maneuver performed in many role playing games, especially the Hero System, where the character loses points from their statistic called endurance. Move tends to tire out the character thus making the character easier to defeat.

Flame War: n *Internet* a heated argument on internet forums and web sites that lead two or more individuals to engage in name calling or personal attacks on the other instead of the topic being discussed.

Foreigner: n *Music* rock group formed in 1976 by musicians Mick Jones, Ian McDonald and Lou Gramm. Foreigner has had many different members over the years, and reached their biggest success in the late `70's and `80's.

Ghostbusters: n *Movies* classic movie released in 1984 starring Bill Murray, Dan Aykroyd, Sigourney Weaver, Harold Ramis, and Ernie Hudson. Created the phrase: "Who Ya Gonna Call?"

Gimli: n *Fantasy* character from J.R.R. Tolkien's book series *Lord of the Rings*. Gimli was a member of the Durin's folk (or Longbeards), the most important race of dwarves in Middle-Earth. Gimli joined Frodo Baggins quest to destroy the Ring of Power and thus became one of the Fellowship. Gimli was played in the movie adaption of the *Lord of the Rings* by John Rhys-Davies.

Google: n *Internet/technology* American company dealingwith Internet search, cloud computing and advertising technologies. **to Google: v** using the internet search engine to search the internet for some topic of interest: *I Googled Star Wars.*

Goonies, The: n *Movies* classic movie about a group of kids who go searching for hidden pirate treasure in their community. Written by Steven Spielberg and Chris Columbus the movie was directed by Richard Donner and released in 1985. Movie starred Sean Astin, Josh Brolin, Corey Feldman and Jonathan Ke Quan.

Greedo: n *Sci-Fi* Bounty Hunter appearing in *Star Wars: A New Hope*. Greedo attempted to capture Han Solo for Jabba the Hut, but he was shot and killed by Han.

Han shot first: inj *Sci-Fi* A saying taken up by the fans of Star Wars in response to the changes made to the special edition of *Star Wars: A New Hope* where Han Solo is shown shooting in response to the bounty hunter, Greedo, instead of shooting Greedo first as in the original version.

Hulked up: v *Marvel Comics* Way of showing incredible, unnatural strength during a fight. Based on Marvel Comics' hero The Incredible Hulk who could get stronger the madder he got. Professional wrestler Hulk Hogan employed the technique near the end of all of his matches.

iPod: n *Technology* portable media player designed by Apple started in 2001. iPods can be used to download and listen to music as well as games, videos, television programs and e-mail.

Jumped the Shark: v *TV* term used to indicate when a beloved television program has done something that it cannot recover from and has thus started the downward path in quality. Named after the infamous episode of *Happy Days* where the Fonz actually jumped real sharks on water skis.

Justice League of America: n *DC Comics* super hero group sometimes abbreviated JLA. The roster varied over the years but the classic group included such big wigs as Superman, Batman, Wonder Woman, Green Lantern, Flash, and Green Arrow among others.

Lady Gaga: n *Music* American pop singer born Stefani Joanne Angelina Germanotta. Her record "Bad Romance" was a chart topping success.

Mentalist: n *Role-Playing Game/Comics* a term to describe someone who can use the powers of the mind. Powers generally include mind control, telekinesis, telepathy, clairsentience, among others.

Nakatomi Plaza: n *Movies* location of the terrorist takeover in the movie *Die Hard*. Nakatomi Plaza was a business building found in Los Angeles, California. In real life, the skyscraper in called Fox Plaza and is 492 feet high with 35 floors.

Nerf Herder: n *Music* pop punk band from Los Angeles who describe themselves as a playing "geek rock." They are probably best known for playing the theme song to the television show *Buffy, the Vampire Slayer*.

O'Connell, Jerry: n *TV/Movies* actor who starred in TV program *Sliders* as Quinn Mallory, and the movie *Stand By Me* as Vern Tessio. O'Connell also voiced Captain Marvel in the *Justice League* series and starred in CBS's *The Defenders*.

Ook Ook now fire: n *Music*line from Paul and Storm's song *Me Make Fire*. The song tells the story of the first caveman to create fire and the "accidents" that went with it.
Ook Ook now fire after trying to hide beneath a bear skin.

PnP: n *Role-Playing Games* stands for Paper and Pencil. Term is used to distinguish between role-playing games and role-playing video games.

Qui-Gon Jinn: n *Star Wars* character from *Star Wars: The Phantom Menace* played by Liam Neeson. Qui-Gon Jinn was Obi Wan Kenobi's Jedi master and was responsible for finding Anakin Skywalker who would eventually become Darth Vader.

Risk: n *Games*made by Parker Brothers, Risk is a strategic board game where players attempt to take over the world by moving your armies across the board and achieving "world domination."

RPG: n *Role-Playing Games* abbreviated term for role-playing games.

Sallah: n *Movies*a reoccurring character from the Indiana Jones series of movies, Sallah in an ally of Indy. Sallah is an Egyptian excavator and was portrayed by John Rhys-Davies.

Scooby Doo Mysteries: n *TV* Any number of animated series that follow the adventures of Scooby Doo and the kids that follow him. A Scooby Doo Mystery would be known for creepy old houses, fake monsters, and bumbling crooks foiled by the group of kids and their dog.

Scooby Gang, the : n *TV* **1.** The gang from the *Scooby Doo* series' over the years including Scooby Doo, Shaggy, Velma, Fred and Daphne. Some may include Scrappy Doo or Scooby Dumb. **2.** Group from *Buffy, the Vampire Slayer* that would help Buffy Summers on her battles with the forces of darkness. Included characters such as Xander Harris, Willow Rosenberg, Rupert Giles as well as Oz, Spike, Anya, Dawn Summers, and others over the years the series ran.

Skywalker, Luke: n *Star Wars* main character from the original trilogy of *Star Wars* movies, Luke was played by Mark Hamill. Star Wars episodes IV-VI dealt with the trek of Luke becoming a Jedi Knight like his father.

Sliders: n *TV* television program that ran from 1995-2000 about a group of people traveling from alternate earths through a process called "sliding." Starred Jerry O' Connell, John Rhys-Davies, Cleavant Derricks and Kari Wuhrer.

Spectre, the: n *DC Comics* powerful, ghostlike character from the DC Universe. Originally a man named Jim Corrigan, his spirit returned to seek vengeance. Spectre has taken several forms over the years including that of Hal Jordan (Green Lantern)

Storm: n *Marvel Comics* Orroro Munroe. Storm is a member of the X-Men, acting at times as a leader of the team. Storm has weather control powers. She first appeared in *Giant-Sized X-Men #1*. She has recently married the Black Panther.

Two-Face: n *DC Comics*   Harvey Dent was Gotham City's DA until an accident scarred half of his face as well as his psyche. Two-Face uses a two headed coin with scars on one side to determine what he does, leaving major choices to fate. One of Batman's rogue gallery.

Thor: n *Marvel Comics* Based on the Norse mythology's God of Thunder,

Thor is one of Marvel Comics most powerful beings. Thor carries his mystical hammer, Mjolnir. Thor is a member of the Avengers and he has super strength, flight, control over lightning, and can open a dimensional passageway to Asgard.

Ultimate Nick Fury: **n** *Marvel Comics* Based after Samuel L. Jackson, Nick Fury got a makeover when the Ultimate line of comics came out. Nick Fury was changed from a middle aged white man, to an African American. Both versions have an eye patch over their left eye.

Underdog super energy pill: **n** *TV* a pill that cartoon character Underdog hid in a "secret compartment of his ring" that he would take when in desperate situations. The pill would give him the energy jolt needed to overcome the villains.

Vampire; The Masquerade: **n** *Role-Playing Games* an RPG where player characters are vampires attempting to hide their existence from humans in a setting called "The World of Darkness."

Venkman, Dr. Peter: **n** *Movies* lead character in the *Ghostbusters* series of movies, played by Bill Murray. Dr. Venkman is a parapsychologist. In 2008, Empire Magazine named Dr. Peter Venkman one of the 100 Greatest Movie Characters of All Time.

Venom: **n** *Marvel Comics* Spider-man villain. Venom is covered by the black costume that Spider-man brought back with him from the *Secret Wars* Limited Series. The costume was revealed to be a symbiote,and Spidey got rid of it, but the costume found Eddie Brock and Venom was born.

Weird Al: **n** *Music* "Weird Al" Yankovic is the master of parodies and humorous music. Weird Al has been making music since the late '70's. Gained great popularity with a parody of Michael Jackson's hit *Beat It*, which Al changed into *Eat It*. *White and Nerdy* is a staple of geek music.

Wikipedia: **n** *Internet* web site that acts like an on-line encyclopedia. Wikipedia can be edited or changed by anyone with access to the site. This has led to doubt about the verifiability of the site.

Willis, Bruce: n *Movies* American actor who has starred in numerous action/adventure movies over the years such as the *Die Hard* series, *The Fifth Element*, *Sin City*, *Pulp Fiction*, as well as the critically acclaimed *Sixth Sense* among others. Originally starred in the classic TV show, *Moonlighting*.

Xander: n *TV* Xander Harris is a character from the TV show *Buffy, the Vampire Slayer*. Xander was played by actor Nicholas Brendon for the entire run of the series.